THE TROUBLE WITH BOYS

COURTNEY VAIL & SANDRA J. HOWELL

Sandra J. Howell

THE TROUBLE WITH BOYS

COURTNEY VAIL & SANDRA J. HOWELL

WEST RIDGE FARM PUBLISHING
Hampden, Massachusetts

Published by West Ridge Farm Publishing in Massachusetts
Cover Design: Amy Rooney
Cover Photo: Shutterstock

Publisher's Note: This novel is a work of fiction. Names, characters, places and incidents are either products of the author's imagination or used fictitiously. All characters are fictional, and any similarity to people living or dead is purely coincidental.

ISBN-13: 978-0-9845582-4-7 (West Ridge Farm Publishing)
ISBN-10: 0984558241

Printed in the United States of America

Dedicated to

horse rescue farms

and therapeutic riding programs.

Kat

Hi, I'm Kat. I like that my nickname goes perfectly with my animal-loving nature. Horses are my passion, and it crushes me to know there are way too many like Cinnamon, the gorgeous mare I was currently grooming, that need to be rescued. We have room here at my farm Sunnybrook where I live. It's not like I want the moon—Gru from *Despicable Me* already tried that—just, please pretty please, *one* more. Just one. It would make a huge difference, especially to the horse.

I begged God with my most earnest plea, but my mom won't budge. Her insistent, "No way, Kat," haunts my dreams. Wait. Wouldn't that be *nightmares*? Yeah. Yes! It gives me nightmares! Horrible, ugly nightmares. All I picture while lying in bed is some too-skinny horse munching up grubs because that's all it has to live on, and it's crying out for *my* help. Maybe God'll send an angel to wind-howl, "One more," into Mom's ear, convincing her to cave, or someone'll just roll in here with a trailered present that she absolutely cannot turn away because it has nowhere else to go.

An empty stall taunted me next to where I had Cinnamon clipped at the crossties. I winced at the pricker-bush anguish overtaking my lungs. And trust me, I know *all* about prickers after last week's solo woodland excursion that I totally bombed while trying to outdo my frenemy River, who's part hound dog and a whole lot Cherokee. Yeah, like I said, I *bombed*, in glorious tumble fashion, collecting the sweet mementos of four baseball-sized bruises and pricker scratches, lest I forget my stupidity.

I ran the curry brush in circles down the American Paint horse's silky side. "Rescue's *so* important," I told Aisha, the ten-year-old working with me. She's learning to ride while her twin brother Devon takes lessons in the therapeutic riding program. "Some horses are abandoned or some have health issues that become too burdensome. With others, their owners can't take care of them anymore for financial reasons or a boarding issue. I really want to take in *more* rescues, but, my mom hates the idea."

In our therapeutic riding program, we teach kids to

groom, and ride if they can, and Aisha wanted to learn everything about horse care and was loving every bit of this. Her brother with ADHD? Yeah, not so much. He often went all stink-faced, complaining about how horses are so dumb. Lately, boys have been getting on my last nerve.

"The lovely Cinnamon here," I continued, "was brought in last November when she was about to foal."

"What's *foal?*" Aisha said, stopping her brushing to scratch her light brown arm that Cinnamon whisked with a flip of her cream tail.

"Oh, have a baby. *Two* horses means more work, expenses, etcetera, etcetera." I forgot she wouldn't be all up on horse terms. "Well, you've seen her baby, the feisty Flash. I got to help with the birth. My first time. It was so gaggifying yet beautiful at the same time. Flash has so much energy. He's like the wind and won't stay still."

"Sounds like my brother."

I laughed. "Yeah. Maybe that's why Flash is the only horse Devon likes. River and I have been trying to calm Flash down, and now that he's weaned, which means off his mother's milk, we might pony him with Jacinda's horse, Angel. It's kind of a buddy system with a better-behaved horse acting like a good example, and Angel's so calm, patient, and sweet that she's perfect for the job. Horses have to learn to do what the rider wants rather than what it wants while under saddle. Being led beside Angel while she's being ridden will give Flash the sensation of being directed and ridden by a person. Flash will hopefully get in sync with Angel, following the commands of her rider, most likely River. With lots of practice, the younger horse should get the gist. That's my hope with Flash anyway."

"I'd love to ride Flash. Can I, if it works?"

"Well, Flash is still a baby. A horse has to put on body mass, learn commands, and get used to a bridle and a saddle before it can be ridden, and it takes a couple years at least."

"A couple years?" she cried. "I don't know if I'll be here that long."

"I don't know if Flash will be either," I muttered.

"Aww. That stinks. Well, I think I'll stick with Angel then, when I can get her. I love her, but she's popular. Ginger's my next favorite. I got to ride Angel last week. I love her curly mane like long strands of white twisty macaroni."

"I know. You should see her in winter. Her coat gets wavy too."

"Wow. Really? Cool."

"*She* was a rescue too. Jacinda, my BFF, mostly worked with her, as I'm sure she's told you 'cause she loves to brag about Angel's brilliance and show off her circus tricks. I wasn't too keen on her at first because she was so weird-looking and scrawny, but her sweetness eventually sucked me in too. I wanna take in more rescues, but my mom doesn't think I can handle the responsibility. I *can*, I know it. If Jacinda can do it, then so can I. I've grown up with horses."

As if on cue, her Spidey senses tingling, my mom came in. Not hearing her approach like I did, she startled Aisha when she said, "Hi, girls. Whatcha doin'?"

"Hi, Mom. Just grooming Cinnamon. Need help somewhere else? We're almost done with her."

"No. I'm gonna take some pics of her when you two are finished."

Knowing exactly what that meant, my hand froze in place and my stomach dropped. "You're putting her up for sale?" I asked, trying my best to say it as cool as possible, but it came out all cracked.

Before I could blink away the puddles in my eyes, they fell in uneven streams down my cheeks, just to echo my mom's number one reason for not wanting me to take in rescues. She thinks I'm too *soft*. She'd say big-hearted 'cause she's nice like that, but I know she means *soft*, AKA *wimpy*.

"You knew this was coming, Kat," she said, with that stinging tone of 'I told you so' because she spotted my blabbermouth tears. "Getting so attached is why rescue puts us in a tough spot. We end up loving the horses we work with. We can't keep them all."

I wiped my cheeks quickly and pivoted with the brush still in my hand. "I know. I know that. I'm *not* too attached. I was just thinking about poor Flash. He's just a baby."

"He's weaned now. He'll be okay without his mom."

"River will not like this," Aisha said with a shake of her head. Her full bouquet of springy black curls bounced in her insistence.

"River doesn't get a say," my mom said. "He's just a volunteer here."

Hoping to prove my responsibility and gain some cred back because my dumb tears had made mush out of me, I said, "River and I are gonna pony up Flash with Angel. Hopefully, that'll calm him down."

"Excellent idea. If we can have both horses out of here by the Fall Fundraiser, that would take a load off my mind, not to mention my pocket. Maybe we'll work to sell Flash at the event. If he's calm enough to sell, that could bring in some interested buyers, as well as other horse lovers who are inspired to donate to the program."

Man, ice dagger to the chest. Ugh, I suddenly felt sick. That's *so* soon. That gives us... I tried to crunch the numbers, okay, not *crunch*, count the weeks from here. Mid-August to the third weekend in October? That's um

… aw crud buckets! I need a calendar! Eight? Nine weeks? Cinnamon'll be snatched up soon, maybe by next week. She was a dream. But we only had a handful of weeks left with Flash? I liked Flash, even though he was wild and zany. He does have a sweet heart and a playful spirit. But River, oh my goodness, River LOVED Flash. They're close buds. My mind began reeling. "When Cinnamon sells, can we take in another rescue? Just one? Please? Maybe after the fundraiser?"

"They're a huge responsibility, Kat. You know that. We have more kids now than ever and don't have the extra volunteers to lend to a rescue program."

"I know. But there are just so many in need. River and I have been doing awesome. I have people asking all the time if we take in rescues, and it breaks my heart to turn them all away."

"We *don't* take in rescues. Your father brought home Angel, and Cinnamon was an emergency situation. Of course I'm not gonna turn away a mare about to foal. Word got out about Angel, so now everyone wants to drop off the horses that they can no longer take care of. But this is a therapy and riding lesson farm, Kat, *not* a rescue farm. Plus, the attachment thing. You just cried over Cinnamon when you've always known she'd be put up for sale after Flash's weaning."

"I know, but Flash just got pulled a few weeks ago. I

didn't have time to get my mind in a sale mode. You sprung it on me out of nowhere."

My mom crossed her arms in her unmovable stance of NO and sighed, glancing at Aisha, then popped her gaze back to me. "We've already discussed this, but we'll pick this conversation up again later."

What's the point. You've already made up your mind. "No. I get it, I guess. Let's … get this girl camera-ready and help her look her best."

"That's the spirit. Thank you for being so mature about this."

"Sure." Well, I'm no baby. I only get attached because I care so much. But I can be cool. I can. Totally.

When Aisha and I were done grooming Cinnamon, we unclipped her and led her out to the big corral so my mom could take some shots of her in the sunshine to show off her interesting paint marks. Even though she was good-to-go, I was still fussing and running my fingers through her silky, cream-colored mane. I liked perfection. So many things were art to me.

"Mom, be sure to get a couple close-ups because she has such pretty eyes." Her eyes were so feminine with huge lashes that she almost looked like a cartoon. In fact, I was inspired by Cinnamon and created a comic strip just for kicks. It's all about a girl and her horse. My besties Jacinda and Emily love it and find it hilarious. It shares the funny misunderstandings people have about horses and teaches truth in a humorous way.

I let go of Cinnamon's lead line and stepped away so she'd be solo.

My mom walked around Cinnamon, taking pictures from different angles, and she pulled back to get some full-body shots. "Wonderful grooming, girls. She looks spectacular."

"Thanks. What are the pictures for?" Aisha asked.

"They'll go on the website," I said. "And I'll put them on our Facebook page."

"I'll also start posting some listings online tonight," my mom added.

"Oh," I clipped. "Tonight?" My mom was totally serious about time. "Wow. Great." That didn't exactly sound full of conviction. It fell flat and limp like a farting balloon losing air.

When my mom was finished, she waved goodbye and walked back towards the house.

"Bye, Mrs. M!" Aisha called. When my mom was out of earshot, she frowned and said, "River'll be *so* upset, I know it."

"He will. How do you know so much about River? You keep mentioning him."

"Well, I'm in his club. Devon too. I know him from that. He talks about Cinnamon and Flash all the time."

"What? What club?" I fell into a fit of boisterous laughter, crossing my arms. "River has a club now? Like what? Learning how to tell the age of a bear by its poop pile?"

"Not exactly. We're Earth Helpers."

I stopped laughing and gawked. "Earth Helpers," I muttered, with the itch of annoyance. I scrunched my lips. That sounded a little like an Angels Club knockoff, if I'd ever heard one.

"We mostly work a community garden at his farm. And we recycle and upcycle. River also volunteers for the state park and marks the trails for hikers. It's just me and his friend Greg and Devon. River's other sidekick Sly won't garden or be in our club because it's supposedly a *girl* thing. But, we pick up the slack where your club leaves off."

Uh huh huh huh. I recoiled as if I'd heard wrong. "Excuse me? Where my club leaves off? What's *that* supposed to mean? He thinks his little club is competition? We *help* people! *Lots* of people."

"We help people too. But in a different way than you."

"Pick up the slack? That's *his* phrase, I know it. He tosses fancy words around like confetti. What is he, a cult leader? What is this garbage he's spewing about my club? He knows nothing."

"No, he's not a cult leader, silly. The garden pulls

people in the community together. It gives fresh fruits and veggies, along with our fresh farm eggs, to the poor. We also try to teach people green ideas. Does *your* club do that?"

I gawked then ground my jaw and clenched my fists. Oh! My! Glowing! Stars! I didn't answer her because, in truth, it kind of didn't. Not yet.

The vortex of fury swirling up in my mind was heading straight for River Redstone. Slack? Are you kidding me? How dare he! Who does he think he is? We do not have slack. We just haven't gotten to all our ideas yet. What we have now, my friends, is WAR. Bloody, ugly, brutal war. And he declared it with all his "slack" talk about my Angels. Ridiculous! Well, he messed with the wrong chick. You don't trash my club and come out with a clean shirt. No way. And River and his little ragtag band of veggie-tree-loving peeps is gonna flat-out lose. You can be sure about that. Just wait 'til my Angels find out about this. They'll be equally furious. Slack? Whatever. Err, just wait 'til I find that thieving traitor and give him a piece of my mind. If he wants to be our competition, we'll show him good game all right. And win!

2

River

Being *River*, you'd think holding a name after a body of water would give me some additional charm to call for rain through dance. Nope. I couldn't even jerk mist out of the clouds with my very best moves. Okay, maybe line dancing didn't exactly count in the ancient art, but I tried my best. All for nothing though.

While I was pushing the wheelbarrow from the big barn to the small barn at Sunnybrook Farm, purple-black clouds rolling in overhead snagged my gaze. I was riveted, even as the demonic-looking puffs suddenly lost grip on the water they were carrying. Yes, rain! Finally! I smiled and tilted my face up. "Yes! Thank you!" I cried out.

Raindrops smeared down my cheeks and outstretched arms like wet, slobbering kisses from my choco lab Jack. In no time at all, the random kisses turned to torrents of rain that came in plenty and exploded in cold, liquid bursts when they collided with my sweaty skin. The water's intensity as it dumped from the sky amazed me. It pummeled and sopped everything within my visibility in a whooshing rush. Woodland animals probably scuttled for cover, but I stood there like a scarecrow, relishing nature's shower. I've never hated the rain or snow storms. It had been hot and dry for two weeks, increasing the risk of fire in the state park and the surrounding woods that ran up behind Sunnybrook Farm, so this gift was definitely needed, not only for that but my club's community garden.

I was drenched in ten seconds flat. It truly seemed like the gloomy clouds held buckets of water that poured every bit of their treasure trove onto this thirsty land.

No way could I bike home in a downpour like this. My mom'd kill me. I can hear the worry in her voice now. "If you see lightning, River, remember to count from the moment it lights up the sky until the crash of thunder. For every five seconds in between, the storm is one mile away. So take cover before it reaches you." Of course I know that, duh. She's drilled it into my head since I was four, and I'm almost fourteen. But she still reminds me all the time. Crud. I'll have to wait it out in the barn so she won't go ballistic. My mom's great aunt was struck by lightning when my mom was a kid, so she's obsessed and has a major phobia, hunkering under covers, as if that would help. When I was little, she'd cover me with blankets too, and we'd huddle in a corner of the room, and she'd tell me all about the earth and animals until the storm passed. She'd often try to cheer us both up by pointing out how much better we had it compared to our ancestors who were forced to pack up and move thousands of miles from their land in Georgia when gold was discovered in 1828. I felt so sad to learn how at least 4,000 Cherokee lost their lives in the gaping, heart-wrenching scar in our heritage known as the Trail of Tears.

I, on the other hand, have always found storms fascinating.

Tucking back into dry shelter, I wiped my face and squeezed my curled-up shirt in my fists as I listened for thunder and squinted to spot crackling flashes across the sky. Those gems should've been there, but there was only the wild, pounding drumbeat of water on the wood. It was weird to have such storm-like rain without the thunder and lightning I loved. Water gushed by the side of the barn and mud flowed towards the smaller barn next to the indoor arena. Without the danger of lightning yet, I considered gunning it in a speedy ride home, but there was no way I wanted to risk getting grounded. Our dippy, country roads didn't have storm drains and were probably already flooded in spots, even in just the few minutes of the downpour. However, I liked to be respectful of my mom's feelings, even when she was being completely and utterly ridiculous and over-anxious.

I'll just wait it out or call her if it doesn't let up. At least I can chill with the horses. I love volunteering here. I get to be near and even ride these spirited creatures. The sound of pounding hooves danced in my head in the stillest moments.

Horse passion is the only thing that gnat Kat and I can agree on. We usually put aside our differences and try to work as a team for the benefit of the two rescues we loved so much, but we argued about everything almost all the time. Art, sports, trails, the best way to do certain things. Dang, even music! I love country and southern rock, while she loves Christian and pop. I don't mind *some* uplifting stuff, but I like me some twang and a line-dancing, toe-twisting beat.

Back in the bowels of the big barn, the scent of the fresh shavings I just raked into the stalls lingered in the cool, damp air. Smells of leather and horses intermingled with grain and sweet hay. I drank it in with a deep whiff. There was nothing like the blended aroma of a horse barn. Okay, my mom's kitchen was a close tie, but still, this was one of the best. Someday, I hope to have my own farm and horses.

My small four-stall barn at home was currently empty.

I wished with all my might I had the money to buy Flash, but I didn't. Not even close. I've got $285 or something like that in savings and some chump change here and there and that's it. Now that Flash's mom's on the market, I'm sure Mrs. M's gonna put him up for sale as soon as he's less jumpy. As much as it's tempting, I can't cheat in the process either. There's no way I'd ever compromise a horse's well-being just so I could get—at *most*—a couple more months of bro time with my bolt of joy. If I'm lucky, I'll have 'til about Christmas to work up my strength to let him go. He'd make a wonderful present for some lucky kid, but, sadly, it won't be me.

I do have some other equine friends here too. Mrs. M lets me ride whichever one I want for free, whenever I want, in exchange for my help around here. Most days I ride Kerry, this lovely bay Morgan mare now pleading with her eyes and vocal prattles to help ease her anxiety. Kerry had her head over the stall door. I stroked her soft face and mane and gave her the last baby carrot I had in my pocket. She ate it and bobbed her head, inviting me to give her more soothing attention. I scratched her neck. She was scraping her hooves and gave a low-pitched neigh in nervousness. She was feisty enough for me. I like 'em a bit wild 'cause people don't wanna ride them as often. I have a heart for rejects and underdogs. That's why I love Flash so stinkin' much. Kerry had her issues, but I've worked with her a lot over the past year, and she's chill enough now that she's used in therapy too, not just for lessons. When one of the therapy kids is riding, she can sense it and is a totally different horse. She's no Angel, who's cuddly and warm. Kerry's a bit aloof, but the kids in the program can lead her easily and she's gentle and steady doing a smooth trot with a student on her back.

My mom thinks my natural kinship with horses comes from our Cherokee heritage. I don't know about that. How could anyone not love them? They're so graceful and powerful and they love to connect with their riders. Riding a horse was inborn and effortless for me. When on the back of one, no matter what horse, I felt one with it. "It's okay, girl. No scary noises yet. Learn from Angel over there. See how still and calm she is?"

Angel nickered when I said her name, trying to nudge a veggie out of me no doubt.

"Sorry, Angel. Last carrot." I wiggled my empty fingers but walked over and gave her a cookie from my pocket. Cinnamon spoke up too, neighing that she wanted one. "Of course Cinnamon wants one too now. See what you did, Angel? Contagious hunger. Now, I gotta make the rounds." I gave Cinnamon a cookie and scratched her nose.

Can't believe Kat didn't tell me! I'm so annoyed. I had to see it on the Facebook page that Cinnamon was put up?

Man. That was fast. Haven't even seen Kat today. She didn't text me about it or anything. Rude much! She'd better not do that to me with Flash. I'd likely never forgive her. But a countdown clock was ticking. Its loud clicks jackhammered in my brain, telling me it was only a matter of time before he was ripped away from me forever.

The rain eased off to a softer sputter and then stopped.

Sucking in a deep breath, I peeked out and glanced up at the separating clouds. The air smelled good and clean, and the wet landscape glistened. "See? No storm, Kerry, just a passing, heavy rainfall. It's all cool. Fooled us both. I'll have to prob'ly carry my bike home, but I'll see ya tomorrow."

I stepped out and balanced the barn rake across the wheelbarrow, then walked it to the back of the small barn holding the boarders and Flash. I pulled a horse cookie from my pocket and fed it to the black Appaloosa, Chico, one of my favorite horses here. Aw, who am I kidding? It's too hard to pick my favorite. They're all so different and amazing, even Kat's horse, Sassy. The other two horses in the stalls next to Chico, begged for their treats, and Flash did too. I'm glad Flash has settled in with his new friends at this barn since he'd been weaned and pulled away from his mom.

I smiled as I stopped at each stall and gave them

cookies. I spoke to each and rubbed their heads. "Okay, you guys. I'm done. See ya tomorrow." I was glad for the blanket of wetness, even though the road was probably deeply puddled. The forest, as well as my garden, needed this big gulp. My farm garden was an important supplier for the Community Cupboard.

With one last glance at the big barn, the thought of Cinnamon up for sale made me queasy and a little mad. Time with Flash was so cuttingly short. There was more than enough room at my barn that my grandfather kept clean and maintained. But I certainly didn't have money to buy him. There was a small field that could be fenced, perfect for him. Visions of Flash being mine danced in my head. Him growing up beside me. Me riding Flash. Flash running through the field. Flash in his stall where I treated him with apples and the occasional mint. But that was foolish. I rubbed my eyes and pushed my wet, black hair away from my forehead as I tried to think of a way to earn enough money to buy Flash but came up with squat. A paper route certainly wouldn't cut it. Our flimsy friendship was doomed.

When I retrieved my bike that was propped against the barn and wiped the seat off, I spotted Little Miss Muffet storming up to me with her fists clenched and a scowl on her face. Her boots splatted through the mud, and she didn't seem to care that she was splashing it up in brown fireworks. What was Trouble so mad about? I was mad too, likely *far* more than her, and I beat her to the punch. "Why didn't you tell me Cinnamon was up for sale?"

She pitched her fists on her hips. "Why didn't you tell me about your dumb club?"

"It's not dumb. It provides a lot of food to the poor."

"Oh, gimme a break. Earth Helpers? Are you kidding me? You only started up a club to spite me."

"Yeah, yeah, that's right. 'Cause the world revolves around you. I totally forgot."

"You are specifically trying to compete with my club. Don't even act like you aren't. Telling Aisha we have slack and you're picking it up? Unbelievable. How long have you had that earthy-crunchy, tree-hugging club anyway?"

"I don't know. I didn't mark it down. I was hoping to join yours, but Jacinda shot me down, and I'm a man of action. I'm not gonna waste time on people who don't want or need my help. Others do, and I'm cool with that. So, my grandfather and I started tilling some ground on our land, and we planted stuff in spring. And as it sprouted during the summer, I decided to get some kid helpers. It has nothing to do with you."

"What are you talking about? When was this that you asked? I have no clue what you even mean. You wanted to be an Angel? When? We haven't taken in any boys yet."

"At the Fall Fundraiser last year."

"Last year?" she cried in disbelief.

"Yes, and apparently, she didn't put it up for a vote."

"Yeah, 'cause she probably knows we can't stand each other."

"Right, but at least I'm mature enough to put our differences aside when I have to for the good of others. It's your loss that you don't accept boys or more people for that matter. Aisha's a crafty little elf. Did you know that? No, probably not, because you Angels are shut down for new applicants, which is nuts. My mom's been teaching her how to make dream and sun catchers that we sell and she's eager to learn and is an excellent gardener now too. I'm not exclusive like you are. My club accepts anyone who wants to make a difference. No one has time for your kiddy games. Grow up. There are homeless people on the streets. Get with the program."

"Don't you dare tell me to grow up. We are very responsible and do a lot of good for people."

"No doubt. But not enough. So that's where the Earth Helpers come in. Hence, the '*slack*'."

"Hence? No one says hence. What are you, Shakespeare?" She gritted her teeth and I smirked, knowing she had no good comeback. She knew I was right.

"But let's get back to the more important question of this heated discussion. Cinnamon. When did your mom put her up for sale? Did you not think I'd want to know about it?"

"Yeah, I figured you'd want to know, but I was livid about all your "slack" talk to Aisha about my Angels. My mom took the pics and put the word out just yesterday."

I sucked in air and it skidded down my throat, making me cough. "What ... will this mean for Flash?" My chest hurt, like a knife plunged into it, and I clutched my ribs. I scrunched my lips because they started to tremble and I furiously blinked moisture out of my eyes so I wouldn't cry in front of this girl I couldn't even stand on most days.

"It's not good news," she said with a frown and a softer demeanor. "I'm sorry."

My voice cracked as I said, "Are we still gonna be ponying him with Angel?"

"Yeah, of course, but my mom wants us to try to get him ready for the Fundraiser."

"What? Are you kidding me? That's like nine weeks at most!"

"I know. My mom wants us to try to get Flash ready for that weekend. She knows it might take longer, but she wants us to aim for that and work with him as much as possible because interested buyers are potential donors for the therapeutic program."

No, no, no. Not so soon. I wasn't ready or prepared for this slam of awful news. I shook my head and turned away from her as I smeared the heel of my hand roughly over my lips and then each leaky eye socket. This was a total nightmare, and my gut burned with as much agony as when my grandmother died this past February.

Flash was awesome. There was no way he wouldn't sell. There was absolutely nothing I could do here. I was losing *my* horse, my very own kin-spirit, Flash. In nine weeks.

3

Kat

The last bit of sunlight on my arms got snuffed out and darkness fell over the pasture at my farm like a giant, black sweater had been yanked across the sky. I gasped when I looked up and saw that the normal rain-gray from just a moment ago had indeed become more snarly and evil. What was this, Tampa, Florida? When I went there for vacation once, rain would come from out of nowhere, long enough to drop water crystals everywhere, and then leave just as suddenly. These summer rainfalls were equally crazy and random. First, yesterday's? And now this? The weather man said there'd be a *chance* of rain. These angry clouds were promising it. Poor MoJoe and Flash. So much for a decent turnout.

My neck prickled as the wind howled and wildly whirled branches and my hair. Scrunching my nose at the air's swampy scent and the kicked up dirt and leaves, I shielded my face and eyes with diagonal arms as I made my way over to the horses to lead them back to the barn. Just as cold drops slid down my skin, lifting up goose bumps, wind ripped through the woods with a louder howl. A large tree limb plummeted from high in a tall tree and smashed down on the fence post. Screaming, I dove to the ground in terror and covered my head in case more branches joined it. Oh my goodness! That was feet from me! That almost hit me! My heart sped and my stomach seized. Nothing else fell, thank God. When I found the guts to look, I gawked and tears burned my eyes. The rainfall picked up, totally drenching me.

MoJoe and Flash both bucked wildly and whinnied from the loud smash and crunch of wood busting wood.

Standing on shaky legs, I tried to calm them with soft words, but my wobbly pleas were useless. Too startled for good sense, MoJoe dashed out of the break in the fence for the woods and Flash ran after him. My heart sank and I shrilled. "Oh my gosh! No. No. Stop. Come back!" There were so many dangers out there. Bears. The ravine, which was a steep, rocky valley. The brook! Oh no! The brook was higher and more swollen after yesterday's rain. I saw it when I rode my bike back from Tory's after our emergency meeting. I panicked and screamed for help. My parents were gone. The farm hands too! I think River's the

only one here. River's my only hope! I screamed his name
again and again as I darted across the wet dirt as fast as I
could to find him. I was out of breath within seconds.

I found River in the barn picking up a bale of hay and
dropping it on the storage room floor to clear a spot for
the wheelbarrow. I stood a drowned rat before him. I'm
not sure if my words made sense because they came out
like tangled yarn. My shorts and shirt clung to my pale
skin and water streamed down my legs

"What tree? You're not making sense. What the heck's
wrong with you?"

I ran up to him, my lungs seizing. I bowled over to
catch my breath and spit out, "Flash ... is gone! He's
gone." My face felt tight as I cringed and clenched my jaw
to keep my teeth from chattering and my tongue from
becoming thick rubber.

"Stop!" he yelled. "I can't understand what you're
saying. What about Flash? What do you mean *gone*?"

I jerked in a deep breath and started over. "A tree limb!
It fell on the post in the pasture near where Flash and
MoJoe were grazing. They got spooked and they took off
through the break. They're gone! In the woods
somewhere. Come on!" In my fear, I grabbed onto River's
arm without thinking about it as we ran out, but then let
go in embarrassment because that was, blah, way too
touchy-feely, even for a freak out moment.

He didn't even notice, I'm sure, because MoJoe was moseying back to the good grass like he was all cool now, but there was absolutely no sign of Flash. OMG! My pulse ran frantically and drummed in my ears as I searched the area. I'm sure River was just as scared as I was when he saw only trees like I did. I slapped my head with both hands. "Crud! I don't see him!"

"Where's Flash, Kat? He didn't follow MoJoe back!"

"I don't know, I don't know," I shrieked, sobs blubbering out without my permission.

"Where are your mom and dad?"

"Not here! They're gone! They went to Spencer to pick up some special feed for Cinnamon. I don't have time to explain. It's up to us. No one else is here."

I'd never seen River rattled, and he was choked up and breathing hard like he'd just crushed a ten-mile run. "We *have* to find him, Kat. I'll die if we don't. Come on!"

"We will. You're the best tracker in these parts, you always say."

We hustled MoJoe into his stall, hung up his halter, and dashed for the woods to find Flash. We sprinted past the broken post and rail, heading towards the edge of the field where dense trees hedged a large pasture.

"What direction did they originally go?"

I pointed at a spot in the tree line. "Um, that way!" Rain poured down, soaking me to the bone and turning the ground to thick, goopy mud. "I'm so scared something happened to him, River. He would've been with MoJoe! He would've followed him back, right?"

"Yes. He loves MoJoe. I have this sick feeling in the pit of my stomach."

"Me too. Come on. Faster!" We raced through the brush as fast as we could. Getting pelted by rain and cold was hardly noticeable because my fear was so sharp. We had to find Flash! The wooded area sloped dangerously into that rocky valley where a quick running brook fed into the river that meandered through the town. Flash could be there, trapped on a rock, suffering from a broken leg, or worse, getting swept away in the current as we speak.

River and I skidded in the mud to a sudden stop at the edge of the wood line. I perked my ears, listening for a whinny, foot crunches, or any sign of Flash. The only sound was the rain slapping the leaves and rushing down the rocks of the steep decline.

River cupped his hands to his mouth and yelled, "Flash! Flash! Flash!"

Still no callback from the missing colt.

I wiped my mouth and whistled through my fingers. Flash always came running when he heard my whistle. We trained him well. Whistles and calls from me or River meant an immediate cookie, but there was no response or galloping hoof beats to be heard.

He looked at me with dread in his eyes when we got nothing.

My eyes were watering, but he probably couldn't tell with the rain dripping down my face.

"He'd never leave MoJoe's side," River said, wiping his face. He flipped his just-past-his-shoulders hair back from his eyes with a pass of his spread fingers down his scalp. "And he didn't come to your whistle? Something's wrong, Kat. Really wrong."

"I know! I feel sick. Do you think he broke his leg or something? Or fell into the brook and he can't get out?" Panic yanked huffs out of my lungs. I did not want this guy to see me cry, no way, but I was about to lose it. For some reason, holding back tears, which could easily be chalked up to raindrops, was much easier than the harder-to-conceal sobs I had to keep gulping down.

"Hope not. Even with the rain and gooey mud, we can't stop looking. We'll have to head down into the valley. If he's hurt, he might not have time for us to wait for a dryer moment." River was using his sharp eyes to look for something, tracks probably. He pointed. "Look! They went through here."

He's been tracking animals since he was able to walk. His grandfather taught him how to notice the trail of clues left by even the smallest animal. Sometimes it was the grass laid flat, prints in a deer path, or a broken branch. They all held signs of the direction an animal or person traveled.

"How can you tell?"

"Look at the bent grass and broken vines. They point in that direction like arrows. And there! Aha. See?" River pointed to the ground. "See those scuffs in the mud made by MoJoe and Flash as they raced down the hill? Different sizes. They're fresh, so it's not from trail horses. It's them. The softer ground from the rain is great for tracking their hoof prints and the trail of kicked-up brush helps too, but it makes our hunt more treacherous."

"Treacherous? Full of danger you mean? Yeah, I hate danger."

"No kidding, Miss Complainer."

"Shut up. You're not as tumbly as me." I sneered behind his back as I followed after him, watching where I stepped so I wouldn't slip and fall. Although I'd never admit it to his boring face, I was glad he was here to help me and that he had stealth and keen tracking skills. If anyone could find Flash, it was River.

When we weren't arguing about who knew the most about horses or just about everything else, if I think about it and suppress the urge to gag, he has kind of become a bestie of mine. He was slowly becoming more friend than enemy in our twisted dynamic.

I was really interested in the tracking methods he

taught me, and this summer, we'd spent countless hours looking for signs of rabbit, fox and deer. But I was still really miffed about his dumb Earth Helpers Club. I ran some recon-spy work to learn what else they were up to. I found out from Aisha they use Cherokee code words. They have a secret language too? Uckkk, can you believe it? Unbelievable! Gag me.

At least my Angels came up with a good plan to out-surpass his club's good will. I can't stand that River stumped me on the food thing, err, but I realized we *do* feed the poor. Not with a garden, but we've done can drives and we put on two picnics for the hungry this summer, with food we cooked up and entertainment we arranged by Posh's cheering/dance squad and Jacinda and Leese playing their music. But hunger's not our sole focus. We care about various social issues. We most definitely do not have slack! No way. On the fly today during our emergency meeting, we created this whole Stand Up Against Bullying campaign as a good comeback, with wristbands and promise pledges that I'm going to present in an assembly soon after school starts. My school already has an anti-bullying program, but this is about helping kids feel inspired and empowered. I already talked to Principal Moran and it's a go. We are in. It's good stuff. That'll put those Earth Helpers in their place and prove once and for all that we do not in any way have SLACK.

A love for horses is pretty much the only thing River and I actually have in common, and an appreciation for nature in general. River loves the stars. I've never really thought much about them to be honest, other than a passing glimpse, but he's been telling me all about Roman mythology and astronomy, which is pretty fascinating.

But all that mattered now was finding Flash.

"Usually, when it rains this hard, it doesn't last long," River said, picking his way through the brush. "Well, at least that's what my mother says."

"It does seem to be letting up a little, but I think that dark cloud is waiting to dump fresh pails of water on us again," I said, looking up at the sky with a cringe.

"Never mind the rain," River replied. "Right now all I care about is Flash."

"Well, me too, duh! Don't be such a jerk. Do you think I don't care about Flash? Don't act like you're the only one who gives a rip here." I bit my tongue and backed off, determined to soften my tone because I did need his help and appreciated what he'd done so far. At least we were heading in the right direction. I had no doubt about that.

We'd been this way before. River loved this wooded valley and made a game out of following the tracks of animals and making me guess which creatures had trekked through. I sometimes nailed it in a good guess, but most often, didn't.

"Horses usually run open paths. They don't like to run through a dense bunch of trees unless they have to," River said, looking down at the ground.

"I know that. I do know horses."

"Well, I'm just *saying* that Flash would've followed MoJoe right through here. Look at the ground."

"I can see their tracks. He did follow him."

He smirked at me. "Wrong. This is where Flash went off a different way. He slipped right there. See those lines in the dirt? Those big dents at the bottom of them show how he tried to climb back up but couldn't get a foothold, so he went down to flatter ground instead."

Annoyed, I scrunched my lips. "Yeah, I knew that."

"Right."

"I did!"

"MoJoe's prints show him circling around and heading back towards the farm. Maybe he came back to get help?" River said, a plea in his voice.

"Maybe," I said, wiping drips from my eyes. "He was sort of nickering." I didn't want to say that MoJoe probably didn't know Flash was in danger and couldn't get back up the steep incline.

We inched our way down the hill. The ground was wet and slick. Downed logs, covered in slippery moss, were not much better.

"Watch out!" River lost his footing on a loose log in

front of us. It rolled and tumbled clumsily down the hill. The wet thing smashed into a million pieces when it hit the jagged rocks at the bottom of the ravine just like my bones could easily do.

I shrilled and recoiled. My heart caught in my throat, and I shuddered. This was not safe in any way. Poor Flash. Poor us. Even if we find him, we'll have to find a less steep incline to climb our way out of the valley. The rain was still pummeling us good, clouding my vision, and making everything soppy and slimy. I have graceless klutz-appeal even on dry, smooth ground. Plus, the heavy cloud cover made this time of day seem like early evening, making it even more difficult to see all that well.

River pretty much locked his gaze to the ground, but every now and then, he'd stop to look for signs to be sure we were going in the right direction as we headed down the hill.

I stayed right behind him, clutching his wet shirt. As we edged down, one careful foot at a time, I didn't care about this awkwardness of contact with our lives on the line here.

I heard a crunchy rustling and saw some streaking beast moving through the thicket. I gulped and my heart jumped. "Huh? Did you see that? Oh my gosh! Was that a bear?"

"No, it was not a bear. It was a deer."

"What if a bear got Flash?" Panic coiled in my stomach. "My parents have warned me about the bears back here."

"Black bears usually go after fish and the bird seed people put out, not colts."

"*Usually* you said. Usually. That means it could," I muttered.

"Well, they can attack what they perceive to be threats or a mama might if she's got cubs, but I'm not seeing any signs of bear here."

"Well, good." When I planted my foot down, I slipped and crashed into River's back. He immediately crouched to catch his balance, bringing me down to my knees. I didn't care about the double splat in the mud. Clinging onto each other for dear life, we both started breathing crazy. Rocks clicked and clacked as they bounced and broke apart on their way down to the jagged bed below. I gulped and coughed in fear. "This is so nuts and dangerous. I'm sorry."

"Careful, careful, Kat. You can do this. You're the strongest girl I know."

"I hope so and that I don't kill you. Or me. I almost … I almost sent you down there like those rocks."

"We're good. We're cool. We're all right." He smeared my dripping hair away from my eyes and my heart stopped for a second. Just stopped. So weird. "We got this. We've been down this way before."

I gulped and pushed that annoyance out to concentrate solely on poor Flash. "Yeah, but never in a downpour."

"We'll live and get our colt back, don't worry. Have faith."

"Yeah, I'll try." I stood and held out a hand to help him up, and we resumed our careful trek down the steep, slippery decline.

I breathed a sigh of relief, and he nudged my upper arm in victory when we made it to the bottom of the hill without breaking our bones or sliding to our deaths.

"See? We did it! We rock!"

"Yeah," I said. "But we don't get that tag until we find our horse." I cleared my throat and quickly let go when I realized I was still clutching his t-shirt as he searched out our direction again.

"This way! Come on!" River jogged along the bank of the brook. "Flash, Flash!"

Keeping a good pace behind him, I heard a sound and grabbed his arm, bringing River to a sudden stop. "Shh. Stop. I heard something. Call out his name again, then just listen." A whinny came from the brook area where the ground sloped down again and rolling, white crests poured over the rocks in a small waterfall. "Yes! Uh, thank God, I hear him! That way, River! Go!" I motioned in the direction of Flash's whinny and felt glad that I was able to lend a useful hand in this search.

River moved swiftly, sliding and slipping along the bank towards the sound of distress.

"Flash, Flash!" River yelled. "He's down near the waterfall of the brook. I see him. By that grove of trees."

The embankment was steep and slick with leaves, forcing us to hold onto small saplings as we planted feet into the slippery mud and skidded over wet rocks on the brookbed.

The closer we got to the small waterfall, the more the sound of the rushing water overwhelmed Flash's whinnies.

At least we knew where he was. We just needed to get to him.

"Flash, Flash!" we yelled in unison as we made our way over to him, so he'd know we were here.

With Flash about ten feet from us now, River and I climbed over the boulders and tried to comfort him with gentle words.

Flash was trapped in vines that had grown and curled their way up and around a thick tree trunk reaching for the sky. Though he looked pitiful, I was so relieved. I let out the breath I didn't realized I was holding in. "It's okay, boy. We're here!"

"Flash's hind hooves are tangled. He's stuck and can't move," River said.

"Did he break his leg?"

"I don't know. Doesn't look like it." River dropped to

the ground beside the frightened colt, and I wrapped my arms around our poor shivering baby.

Flash was soaked to the skin and, although the tree protected him somewhat, rain water dripped down his head. The second I hugged him, he settled down.

If a horse could use a whinny to say thank you, I'm sure this was it when he softly spoke to me and nuzzled my cheek.

Luckily, Flash still had his halter on, so he'd be easy to lead out of here, and we should be able to find flatter ground to walk him. I spoke to him in soothing tones, and River removed his pen knife and began slicing and sawing away at the tangled vines. The usually sassy Flash didn't move. I think he knew we were here to help.

"Hold onto him so he won't accidentally get cut," River shouted out to me.

"I am! Don't worry. I got him. There, Flash. You're gonna be all right. River and I are here to help you. Stand still, boy, so we can get you free."

I was certain the rain was letting up, but it started coming down even worse, which I didn't think was possible, like the sky emptied new pools. "More rain? Are you kidding me? Err, the clouds tricked us!" I sighed in relief when River cut through the last vine and Flash was free at last. "Uh, awesome!" I led Flash over to safer ground. "Come on, Flash."

River stood and ran his hand down Flash's side, then hugged him.

"Is he okay?" I asked, shivering from the cold and my wracked nerves. I was worried he was injured because he was so still and calm. Maybe his energy was zapped from his struggle to get free.

"Yup, except for some cuts on his legs from the vines. But he'll be okay. I'll cut some of this vine, and we can use it for a lead line to walk him back to the farm." He bent down and pulled a long vine up from the muddy brush and cut it. Then he quickly twisted it and looped it through the ring on Flash's halter. "That should work for now."

"Okay, let's go," I said before tackling the slippery the mountain slope.

"Let me lead him on the way up. You'll need both your hands to pull yourself up through the trees. It'll be more slippery going back up. Mud and water are rushing down even faster. I've never seen it rain this hard."

I was about to protest, but when I planted my foot and fell on my palms and one knee, I knew he was right. I did almost shove River off the mountainside with my klutziness before. This was not really a point I could be stubborn on. Rain was pelting my eyes and my boots were full of mud and water. I was going to need both hands.

I gave a little tug, and Flash, feeling the yank on his

halter, came to a stop for me. I was thankful we'd worked with him and taught him to come to a halt with just a slight pull on the lead line. "All right. Here." I had to nibble my lip to shut my mouth as I handed River the vine.

It *was* tricky climbing the mountain, but River was as sure-footed as ever. His ease annoyed me because I was struggling to not land back on my knees. Flash stumbled at times as River led him up the slick mountain.

I followed close behind, hanging onto low branches to stay steady and upright. My worst nightmare would be to fall flat on my face and have him laugh. I'm not sure he would laugh, he's never quite that mean, but just the possibility that he could, not to mention see me looking so pitiful and disastrous, terrified me.

I was so relieved that everything about the way up seemed better than the way down.

And then … we both stopped cold and gasped when we heard the unmistakable, ugly rumble of thunder. He looked over his shoulder at me and I shuddered, not expecting his eyes to have the same degree of worry I knew was booming in mine.

4

River

Flash staggered back and slid down a couple feet when thunder boomed. After steadying the skittish colt, I rubbed his side to calm him and looked back at Kat.

Her eyes held fear when she looked up from the slanted ground she was gingerly hiking up.

"The storm's not close. Hopefully, it'll miss us, but I'm struggling to get him up the hill as it is. It'll be impossible with the thunder. We should find somewhere to take cover and wait it out," I said, stopping at the side of a large tree. Its canopy lessened the downpour on us somewhat, but we were still getting rained on, and any one of these trees could get struck by lightning.

"Like where, Einstein? Some magical cabin? The old lady's shoe?"

"Don't be ridiculous." I ran my hand over my eyes to

wipe drops away. "Um, we could go to the cave and wait there until the thunder stops."

"The cave? Are you crazy? My dad said to never go in there because bears could be in it."

"Flash almost fell here. At another spook, we all could slip down or one of us could get hurt or break a leg. We need to go somewhere safer. And the cave is it."

"Hmm, waiting here to get zapped? Shattering on a bed of rocks? Entering a den of beasts and getting a stern warning on how we, too, can prevent forest fires, right before Smokey eats us? Fun pick. It's like the Wheel of Misfortune. Big money. Big money! Come on. Big spin!"

I loved her sense of humor and sarcasm. "Kat," I said, after a laugh at her comment, "trust me. The cave's the best option and the perfect spot to rest and wait for the storm to pass. I explore it all the time, and I've never seen any bears. It's safe, and better than trying to go further and risk getting Flash or us hurt every time there's a boom or white crackle. Besides, we need to get out of the rain."

She wiped her face and peered around, her hand shielding her eyes. "Where is it even? We've gone this way and that, and I have no clue where we are."

I pointed the direction. "That way."

"Yeah, that helps a bunch, thanks."

"It's too hard to explain, Trouble, but it's down that way. Follow me." I didn't hear her behind me, and pursed

my lips when I spun at her stubbornness. I shouted.
"Come on already!"

"All right! I'm coming! Shut your pie hole, Tracker." A
frown of worry crossed her face.

I shook my head before I turned away from her and
eased Flash up the hill. I smiled when Kat's splatty steps
said she was following me as fast as she could. I turned
right where the rocks and boulders were prominent and a
trickle of water rushed down. "Watch out. The rocks are
probably as slippery as the mud."

"I'll bet. Thanks for the tip."

I led Flash between huge boulders, carefully picking
each spot to plant his feet. Kat huffed in breaths of
exhaustion, following close behind, up the rocky slope.

When I spotted the cave in the distance, I said, "See?
There it is! Over that way."

Kat looked where I pointed. "Dad showed me where
the cave was several years ago when I asked to explore the
property. But he only showed it to me, so I'd avoid it. Are
you sure it's safe? Looks like it's really dark from the
outside. But it's more overgrown with brush now. I never
would've found it again."

"It's totally safe. It's my chill zone. I've got a flashlight,
some matches, and astronomy books in a cooler. Maybe
some Cokes too."

"Your chill zone? You're nuts." I knew I won my

argument when she shrugged. "Better than out here I guess. I hope." She cringed.

"It is. Trust me." I led the way and we carefully passed the towering pines guarding the entrance, which was hidden behind large, rain-crushed bushes and some other wild growth. It was a centuries-old hole in the hillside. The opening did look dark and forbidding.

I wrapped Flash's lead vine around one of the low branches of a sapling under the rock overhang. He was no fan of dark, small spaces, so there was no way he'd come in with us, but at least now, he was out of the downpour and wouldn't get struck by lightning. "It's okay, boy. We'll be right in here."

I pushed the bushes and branches back from the opening, parting the way for Kat to step in first.

She gawked and took a step back. "Are you out of your flipping mind?"

I chuckled and chided, "That's the going rumor."

"Not surprising. *You* first."

"Fine." I went in first and pivoted back to face her then held the dripping brush to the side. "Other than the circus clown with the ax and the fire-breathing dragon, it's all cool." I snickered at the flash of shock on her face that swore she believed me for an instant.

"Hmph, very funny." She crossed her arms.

I turned and held out my hand to guide her in through

the cramped opening. "Would you come on already? There are no bears. I promise." I didn't want to tell her there could be bats deeper in, then she'd huddle up next to Flash and would never come in. I wanted to show off the space. I was sure she'd love it as much as I did, once her shoulders unwound.

"All right." She unlocked her arm pretzel to clutch my hand, and I brought her into my hideaway. Once fully inside with me, Kat bit her tongue, gazing around, still holding my hand with a tight squeeze like she was afraid to let go. I don't think she realized we were still skin-to-skin. *I* did, only because, today, she was no longer that annoying to me and the only touches we usually exchanged were the arm-batting, poking kind. And this was … not horrible. I kind of liked it. We were kind of on an adventure here, and I liked that she was here to share it with me. I liked that she was willing to hike through the woods with me and that dirt didn't seem to bother her. My buddies were just not that into nature. I smiled, watching her take it all in and follow the beams of my flashlight.

She suddenly sneered at our cupped fingers and jerked her hand out of mine.

"What's wrong?" I said, annoyed.

"Eww. Your hand is gross and clammy."

She's *just* noticing? I didn't like her finding me gross.

I'd take stupid or lame over *gross* any day. "So sorry. I just narrowly escaped a near-typhoon."

She patted her thighs and gazed around the walls. "A typhoon? Get real. Exaggeration much?"

"*You're* one to talk."

She shuddered and clutched her chest at a crack of thunder.

Flash whinnied. We both spoke to him to try to calm him down.

I streamed my flashlight around some more and showed her the coolest zone. Beyond the narrow entrance, it opened up to a room-sized jagged wave, like a worm or a warped mouth with four big throats veering off.

Taking the hot spotlight off me and my embarrassment, I quickly spit out, "It's not that scary, Kat. See?"

"Yeah, not too bad I guess. Whoa. There are passageways too? Cool."

"I've checked 'em out a few times but haven't gone all the way back in a while. I know these've been here for decades, but I didn't want to be caught too deeply into the guts if there was a cave-in."

"A cave-in, River? Seriously? You're supposed to be trying to calm me down not freak me out."

The cave smelled musky and damp, even more so because of the last two rainy days.

"I had no clue you came here. I mean, you have a stash

of stuff?" she said, pointing to my cooler. "I don't like you keeping secrets from me. First, your club? And now, this, whole man-cave? You literally have a man-cave."

We both laughed.

"Ah, finally someone who uses 'literally' correctly. So nice."

"Whatever. We're talking about you and all your shadowy dealings. I mean, we're kinda like friends now, I guess. Right? We've been hanging out in the woods together all summer."

"Yeah, we're sorta friends, in the-argue-all-the-time kind of way. I like adventure and the outdoors. You know that. And you do too."

"I'm just stunned you're so familiar with this cave and that you've explored it and whatnot. What's that called? Sputnicked?"

"Haha. Not that. Cave exploring is called spelunking. "

"Right. You did that and didn't even tell me?"

"I don't tell you *everything*. You'd get on my case."

"I would not.

"Right. Want a Coke?"

She chuckled. "Yeah, sure. This is so weird. I can't believe you're offering me a Coke in your heman-woman-hating man-cave." She gasped, shivered and turned her head, staring into one of the dark offshoots.

"What? What's wrong?"

"I think I heard a growl."

"You did. That was my stomach." I laughed. "I only had tomato soup for lunch, so I'm famished.

"Got any snacks? *I'm* hungry too."

"Just some Bugles."

"Bugles? The corn chips?"

"Yep. Better than nothing."

"Yeah, I'll say. Whip 'em out."

I tossed her a bag of Bugles, as well as my zip-up Red Sox sweatshirt from a Zip-lock bag for her to wear. At least one of us could be warmer.

"Thanks," she said with a sweet smile. She slid it on, rubbed her arms, and hugged her chest.

Kat and I sat down on the dirt floor.

I watched Flash to make sure he wasn't pulling on the vine tie. Flash, tired from his stressful day, stood quietly looking at us. "Hey, boy," I called. "You'll be okay."

"Yes, you will," Kat reemphasized. "So, how often do you come here, Mr. Man of Many Secrets?" Kat wiped the drips running down her forehead. Her blond hair was a tangled mess.

"Once in a while. A couple times a month I guess. I've explored the whole place." I ran my hands through my thick, sopping-wet hair, wrung it out, then tied it back in a ponytail with the rawhide string I had in my pocket.

"Now I know what a drowned rat feels like," Kat said as

she removed one of her boots and poured the water out. She leaned over and did the same with the other. She put them back on when they were empty. "Eww, nasty. Squishy, cold socks are the worst."

"Totally agree."

The thunderstorm with its heavy downpour seemed to be letting up and it was definitely getting lighter outside. With my eyes adjusted and the clouds breaking apart, it was light enough in the main area to see what we were doing.

As the rain tapered off, wafts of fog rose from the ground-soaked earth. We wolfed down the Bugles and I gave Flash a couple.

"Look at the fog coming up from the warm ground," I said, stroking Flash's side. I've always loved nature, but Kat taught me to see things with a more artistic eye. "Pretty."

"Yeah. A joy," she said flatly, making me laugh. "I just wanna get outta here and back to my dry home, take a bubble bath, and scrub off these layers of mud."

"We will. Don't worry. The thunder and lightning is far in the distance now. For sure, we'll be able to get back to the farm with Flash. Let's just wait a few more minutes."

"Looks like it's almost over." She sounded so relieved. "Thank God."

"Wanna go further back in the cave and take a look?"

"What about the potential cave-ins? I was actually kind of interested until you mentioned that."

"We won't go far. Just a little further in. There's only one really long tunnel, and we'll skip that one."

"Uh, I don't know." She seemed perfectly fine where she was, gazing around and looking up. "Hey. Check out the weird markings on the walls." She ran her hand over the slimy-looking wall then sniffed her fingers.

"It's nothing I recognize, but I bet the Native Americans from this area knew about this cave and used it, maybe for shelter even." I swiped the flashlight over the walls and got up and moved towards the back of the cave, leaving Kat to either sit where she was or follow me.

"Where ya goin'?" She looked over her shoulder at me.

"I told you. Just deeper in, a little bit. It's fine. You comin'?"

"No, but...what if a big snake slithers out of some crevice while you're gone? You know I hate snakes, other than the little gardeners that I like to spook my mom with."

"Guess you'll have to come along. Don't worry. It's a short tunnel, like twenty feet at most."

"Nah, I think I'll stay here."

"Fine. I'll race back and protect you, if need be. But *I'm* going."

She stood, zipping up the sweatshirt. "I can fend for

myself, thank you very much. Well, as long as it doesn't involve slippery surfaces. Or, like I said, snakes."

"Or bears."

"Right. Okay, okay. I'll go, but I'm bolting if I hear a growl or spot a swoop."

I smirked when she seized the back of my wet shirt and scuffled behind me. There were no bats in this area so I shone the light on the ceiling to show her everything was fine. Hopefully, getting a decent lay of the land would help her to feel more confident and brave.

We reached my favorite part of the cave. A little bit of water trickled down the wall and emptied into a slim channel.

"Turn around, Kat."

"Why?" she said, glancing over her shoulder.

"You can see better now with the light at the opening. It's not so dark out now, so the cave's a pretty cool place, isn't it? Admit it."

"Yeah, it's cool." Dirt crunched under her boots when she pivoted on her toes to look around. "I'm glad you checked it out first. This *is* pretty cool. And that *is* a spectacular view, like something I'm dying to paint."

She was loving it. I knew it! "I know. Nature's poetry."

Sunlight was beginning to punch through the foggy haze with needles of light.

We both sat down in the small space, sipping our Cokes

and looking out of the mouth of the cave at the breaking weather. A calm Flash was nibbling greens. As soon as the streams of light increased, birds starting chirping. The behavior of birds can clue you in to weather changes.

Kat scooted close to the wall and let out a little yelp. "Ow. What on earth is that?" she said, bending her knee and rubbing the back of her calf. "The ground scratched me!" She patted the ground with her hand. "Hey, River! Check it. There's something sharp here. Shine your flashlight here so we can see what it is."

I got up to see.

"Maybe broken glass? No, not broken glass," I said, answering myself, now seeing that it looked surprisingly metal. I bent down, moving my hand over the point of the object, then got down on my knees to get a better look. I'd never noticed anything in the cave other than rock and hard pack. I removed my small knife and started digging in the earth around the pointed corner of the object. "Hey, Kat. Cool! Looks like some kind of buried, metal box. Hold the flashlight, and I'll go and get some sharp rocks so we can dig around it."

"Kay. Hurry back."

I left her and exited the cave to find something to dig with. I stroked Flash's neck on the way out. He was definitely exhausted.

We could leave now because the rainstorm had passed,

but I *really* wanted to dig up the box and see what was in it. I found two angled rocks, grabbed some sticks too, and hurried back to Kat so she wouldn't freak out. I handed one of the rocks to her, then took the flashlight from her and placed it on the ground to beam light into our workspace.

Kat had the look of crazed excitement in her wide eyes as she started to dig.

We worked frantically, laughing. We were so eager. It's just, ya know, you dream of coming across buried treasure in your backyard your whole life, and here we actually found something cool. It could be empty, but since it was buried so deep in the cave, it must've been important to someone, and that made it a treasure to me.

We dug faster and faster until the ground let go of the object.

Kat jerked it up with a big smile on her face and wiped dirt off the top. "What do you think is in here?"

I was itching to know myself. It was so weird to sit around wondering—just jerk the lid up—but I let her relish the thrill of mystery a little longer.

She scratched the lip of the box with her fingernails and gave a good tug. It broke free with a pop and squeaked as she pulled it open.

I licked my lips and grabbed the light.

She frowned and sighed. "Aww bummer. It's just an old

torn shirt or something. Are you kidding me? A shirt? Or…maybe not." After pulling it closer to her face, she threw it in front of mine. "Hey, check it, River. I don't know what this is. Some crude drawing? It doesn't make sense to me, and I'm an artist."

I took hold of it and the disappointment at finding a box filled with nothing but a dumb old piece of shirt zapped when I realized this was so, so much more. "Kat! You know what this is?"

"No clue. I already said that in other words. Would you just tell me already? The suspense is killing me."

"I think … it's a treasure map."

"No, no way. You're out of your mind."

I got closer, shoulder to shoulder with her, and pointed. "No, no, look. Here's the cave we're in. And this wavy line up here is probably the stagecoach road you've told me about. Or maybe the brook?"

"How do you know it's a treasure map though?"

"Because. Way on the edge of it near these three lumps is an X."

"It looks like chicken scratch."

"It's an *X*," I insisted, with a clenched jaw. "Why bury a piece of cloth in here in a box? Why would someone go through the hassle of burying a box in one place and whatever this leads to in another? It doesn't make any sense. Plus, whoever buried it never came back for this. It's still here. So, whatever this leads to is likely still there. This is big, Kat. I can feel it."

She clasped her hands together and hopped once. "Okay, okay, *now* I'm really excited. I actually believe you! This is great. We have our own treasure quest? So cool."

"I know. This is awesome!" My mind was spinning with joy. "We don't have time to look today though. We need to get Flash back and tend to his scratches and give him some hay and water."

"*Riiight*," she said, dragged out with a sneer of suspicion. "You aren't trying to keep it all to yourself, are you?"

"No, no way. I'd never rob you of the stash or the thrill of finding it."

"This is the best thing, River. I never in my wildest dreams would've thought we'd stumble into our own treasure hunt today when we were out risking life and limb to get Flash to safety. Promise me you won't search without me."

I shrugged, "Uh, yeah, sure."

"I did not hear a promise in there." She held out her pinky to me. "Swear to me."

"I am *not* pinky-swearing with you. That's a girl thing."

"Well, you know what I mean. Let's make a pact then, right here and now, that neither one of us will search without the other or say anything to anyone else. It'll be our secret."

"I promise that I will not search or try to decipher the map without you, Kat the Gnat, or blab about it to anyone else."

"And I promise I will not search out the mystery without you, River Scuzface, or tell anyone about it." We made up some hand-twist handshake and shook on it.

"Who's keeping the tin?" I asked.

"*Me*," she insisted with a grab of everything.

"Yeah, figures."

"No. I'm not being selfish. I don't want your dog Jack to eat it. That, uh, that would devastate me."

"Oh, yeah, me too," I said. "Good thinking."

"Wait! If I get caught with the box, then my parents'll want to know where I got it. And I don't want to lie and I honestly don't trust your dog to not eat it."

"Let's put it back in the ground for now and dig it up again tomorrow and we can try and figure it out."

"Okay," she sighed. "Good plan."

We reluctantly put the map and tin back in the ground and covered it back up, then left the dank cave. I tucked the empty soda cans in my cooler to recycle them later. I untied Flash with a swell of hope in my chest and began leading him back up the mountain in the beautiful, cloud-piercing sunshine.

5

Kat

We were busy with farm chores and horse grooming, so forget *one* day. *Three* days dragged by like drowsy snails without River and I getting to search for the mysterious treasure.

I was glad we finally, *finally* got a break and that he was coming over today. Hopefully, we'd discover whatever mystery the map led to. We were on a mission, a *huge* one I could tell. And we kept repeating our promise in texts to not tell anyone, not even our parents or our other friends. It was our secret, our quest.

My parents would probably kill me if they found out I went inside the cave. We didn't really have much choice with the thunderstorm and poor worn-out Flash and all, but still, it could fall either way. I didn't know if they'd be happy about my resourcefulness or disappointed that I dipped into darkness despite my dad's warning. They were already unhappy that we went running down the mountain in the rain, taking a chance with our lives. They told us if a horse escapes again, that we should always wait for them to take care of it and not go searching on our own. Are you kidding me? Not even wild horses could keep River away when Flash was in potential danger. That's like asking Superman to not stop a speeding train from crashing. No amount of explaining about why we took the risk to hunt for Flash changed their minds. They *did* have a point too, but, whatever. What's done is done, and I can't take it back.

But now, we had another reason to go back to the cave. The map.

While we were walking back with Flash after the cave find, River told me before our next search we needed to use unscented shampoo, soap and deodorant since we'll be going deeper into the woods that he hasn't checked out yet. Bears can smell 1000 times better than humans and we don't want to draw them to us. He also said bringing some noise makers so we won't surprise any bears would also be a good idea. Uhh, just the idea of *maybe* seeing a bear freaked me out, but the excitement of hunting for treasure squashed my nervousness.

Of course, *today*, my mom cooked bacon, which I thought would be the absolute worst thing to smell like, so

I put on clean clothes, rewashed my hair outside with the cold water from the garden house, scrubbed it with a towel and put it up in a ponytail. With my hair still damp, I darted into the garage to fetch my mother's garden trowel out of her box, snatched my backpack that I already had in there with a bottle of water, a granola bar and a cowbell, and took off like a Tasmanian devil to meet River at the big barn. I was so super psyched for this treasure hunt … or whatever this was. Maybe we wouldn't find actual treasure, but my chest swelled with the promise of adventure, surely our biggest one yet.

Looking so absolutely 'River' in a tank top, jeans, and hiking boots with a flannel shirt tied around his waist, he was leaning back against the horizontal wooden planks with one foot propped up under his knee and his arms crossed. "Hey," he said with a smile. "Got everything?"

"Yep. I have a million jumping beans and butterflies inside. I'm so excited for this."

"Me too. It's all I've thought about for days."

"I know what you mean."

He quickly folded and wrapped a skull and crossbones bandana around his head, leaving his longish black hair hanging down in back.

"I didn't know we were actually going to be pirates, hunting for treasure. I would've brought my hook from *Peter Pan*."

"We're not. It's hot today and it'll keep sweat and the shorter hair in front out of my eyes."

"Oh, right," I said with an arm scratch, now feeling like a dumb dork. *Pirate, Kat? Really?*

His under-the-breath laugh told me he totally noticed my *gawkwardness.* He tossed his bag over his shoulders and situated it on his back with a wiggle. He tagged me with a light punch to the upper arm, then we took off running in laughter.

He and I ran around the side of the fenced-in pasture and dashed as fast as we could for the woods. We broke through the thick layer of trees and hurdled over downed logs on our way to the valley. We scrambled down the steep slope the best we could. I was surprised to still find it water-logged from the downpour we found Flash in. It's so crazy to think that if Flash hadn't run away and the thunderstorm hadn't forced us to wait it out in the cave, we never would've found the mysterious tin box with the map inside.

"Watch out. It's still slippery going down this part of the hillside," River warned with a shout as he struggled to keep his feet from sliding over a fallen tree branch encrusted in mud.

"I know. I can tell. I'm looking. Don't worry about me. Just lead the way." I caught myself as I almost stumbled over a fallen log. I reached out my hand and snatched a low scrub pine as my feet slipped on a muddy bed of leaves.

"Just a little further. We're almost there." River pointed to the left of the steep decline.

We made our way through the woods, then around the sea of boulders.

As we edged close to the huge gray rocks, a shiver snaked down my spine as I pictured a claw swipe at my face and a deep, angry growl. I clutched my chest with a gasp of terror. "Um, do you think a bear's in there now?"

"No. Trust your instincts. You know how to spot bear tracks from our treks at the state park and the ground is still plenty soft for imprints. See anything that says '*bear*'?"

"Noooo," I whined, truly looking around with a cringe and a keen attention to detail. "No," I said with a nod and a lot more confidence. "I don't see any sign of bear."

"Good little tracker." He turned and patted my head. "They hibernate in the lower caves and don't sleep or live in this cave. I've been in it a dozen times. I told you that. They might look for food further out this way because it's not far from the brook, but being loud and boisterous should help keep them away. The ones I've seen around here are skittish and on the small side."

"*Small* is still two hundred pounds of possible ferociousness."

"Right, but that's why we have to be smart."

River was moving at a swifter pace now and I was doing a decent job staying right behind him, despite my shrimp stature.

Still feeling leery, I said, "When we get there, I'll shine my flashlight in the cave before we go in, just to be sure."

"Fine," he said softly, appeasing me and my silliness rather than making fun.

We trudged to the stand of pines that guarded the way to the cave like big, mighty angels. We ducked under the low branches and edged closer and closer towards it.

River pointed to a bed of needles on the ground. He dropped to one knee and looked closer at the large swath of flattened piles of branches and twigs. "Look, although bears haven't left a mark, deer have."

I watched as he got up and walked around the flattened needle bed.

"See? The deer lay right here, probably during the night. The needles are more compacted and crunched versus loose and random like in the other spots. And look at the deer scat." He pointed to the deer droppings on the ground several feet from the pile of needles. "It's shaped different than bear scat, like an oval pellet."

"Do you think they slept here last night?"

"Yep. Probably during the storm too. The wide, low pine branches keep them dry and help to block the wind. It's kind of like a roof over their head. They don't sleep soundly though. They're always on the watch for predators."

River was kind of amazing and cool when he wasn't being annoying. He sure knew a truckload about animals. And I've been learning a lot from him.

Walking along the side of the hill, River said, "With the deer having traveled across here many times, there's a small path we can follow. It's not as muddy."

I stayed close behind River, and after slipping a few times, we finally made it to the cave. It was so much less scary in the sunshine without the dark clouds and globs of rain. It didn't creep me out today. The bush blocking the opening was broken and my heart stuttered. *Yeah, I think so.* "Was the brush crushed like that last time?"

"Yes. Wait here and I'll go inside and take a look." He clicked on his flashlight and stepped in.

"No way. I'm goin' in too," I said, walking behind him into the dank, dark mountain hole. "You're not leaving me out here."

"Still worried about the bears, huh?"

"Yeah, that, or, ya know, circus clowns with axes."

I clutched River's shirt as we followed his light beam to the part of the cave where the box was buried.

He swiped the flashlight back and forth along the ground and froze the beam on the disturbed patch of dirt. "There it is!" he shouted.

"Yay! Hurry. Dig it up. We can take it outside and inspect the map in the daylight."

River knelt and quickly unearthed the box. He scraped the dirt off the top with my mom's trowel and pried the box out of its resting place and handed it to me. "Here it is. Let's go."

We turned and headed back toward the opening of the cave.

I shrieked, feeling a tickle on the back of my neck.

"What?" River asked with alarm, shining the light in my face.

I sneered at the bright beam. "Something just tickled my neck." I dropped my volume to a whisper. "Do you think it was a ghost?"

"No. Now you're getting crazy," River said. "It's just a daddy long legs, silly." He brushed it off so quickly I didn't have time to squeal again. "Come on. Let's get outta here. I wanna look at the map."

I felt like a major moron. "I'm pretty brave when I need to be, ya know. I can ride the friskiest horses and never let my fear show. But this cave thing has me just a little spooked. All my parents' fault. Too many warnings about the possible dangers everywhere."

"There *are* dangers back here. Your parents care about you and want to keep you safe. We just have to be careful and stay smart."

"I know." I followed him back out of the cave and handed the box to him.

River had it open within seconds and removed the folded cloth. He laid it on the ground, and we both bent over to check it out. "Look here. This upside down U must be the cave. I think this arrow-dash thing shows the way the person took across the brook to hide the map. And it seems like everything else we need to look for to find what's buried is west." He traced the path.

"Does that W mean water or west? Are you *sure* it's west?" I asked, my eyes straining to read the map.

"I think so. On maps it's usually west. I guess we'll have to see. We'll start with west since that's standard. We can tell direction by the location of the sun, but I brought a compass to double check, so let's go west from here all the way down to the brook and follow that to where the approximate X should be. We'll have to be on the lookout for these landmarks." He closed the tin box and set it down under a tree near the cave. "If we don't find anything today, we'll have to come back another time."

"I told my mom we were hanging out today. I know she'll be wondering where we are in a few hours."

"Yeah, and I told my grandfather I'd help him before dinner, so we'd better get going and see if we're lucky enough to find whatever the map shows today."

"But we don't even know what we're looking for," I

said, scrunching my eyes. "Do you think we'll have to dig really deep? We might need a shovel. All I brought was that trowel that's not much bigger than a serving spoon."

He snatched up the box and put it in his pack. "I don't know, but if nothing else, let's just see if we can find the three things that look like some sort of massive boulders."

"The brook is really long, running down the mountain and into the river. I bet things have changed since this map was made. I wonder who drew the map and how long ago it was. It looks very old."

"That's what we might discover, that things are completely different. I hope not. Let's go." River was on the move, working his way down the steep embankment, compass in hand and his focus on the ground.

I stayed close behind him. My friend Posh showed me how to straighten my wavy hair with a frizz free solution, a hairdryer, and a boar bristle brush, but because I'd just put it up today in a ponytail while wet, now that it was dry, my hair's bushy mass of frizz tickled my ears with a pendulum back-and-forth swing at every step.

The going was slow down the steeper part of the mountain, and I saw that River kept eying his compass and then the terrain. He slipped and I grabbed his upper arm to steady him. "Careful, River. Watch where you're going."

"I am. Don't worry about me."

The westward move down the steep slope took time and eventually brought us to the winding brook.

"Okay, let's mark our spot here," he said. "This will tell us where we need to turn to go back up the incline." He found a big stick and embedded it in the ground so it stuck upright.

I looked to the other side of the brook where the mountain sloped upward and met a dirt road that was an old stagecoach route. I remember my mom telling me that Native Americans settled in camps along here. My dad used to take me down to this very spot to watch the trout make their way to the river. He and I used to hunt for treasure like arrowheads and spent countless summer days sitting on the large flat stones with our fishing pole lines dangling in water so we could catch supper. The brook was still running quickly from the rainy days and the level was higher than I'd ever seen it, but luckily, it hadn't flooded onto the bank. The ground was still damp though and our feet squished down, leaving deep imprints in the soft mud.

We resumed our quest and walked and walked. The sun was beating down with warmer rays. I gripped the bottom of my shirt and shook air into it, then swept the sweat off my brow with the wish that I'd brought a bandana too. A little nervous about seeing bears again because we were being a little too quiet aside from our huffy breaths and mud splats, I took my cowbell out of my pack and rang it randomly. He didn't snicker, so I take it, this wasn't such a silly idea, and he took his polished bamboo sticks out and clacked them together to make noise too.

"Look, more deer tracks. Rabbits too," I cried, crouching down to check.

River stopped, but his flatly stated, "Uh huh," said he was more interested in our epic quest than the creature impressions that normally fascinated him. Um, what? Did I slip into another dimension with a completely different River? Even though we had an important mission, I've never known his hawk eyes to rest. Ever. His love for Flash was driving him like a zombie for juicy brains. If we actually did find treasure, real treasure, he might have enough money to buy him, and that would be so jumping-jack amazing. "That's cool, Kat, but we need to focus on the map markings and try to figure out what they mean with regards to the landscape. Do you see any tree or rocks along here that coincide with the four crudely drawn Chocolate Cheerios-looking things at the top above the three, big lumps?"

"No, none that I can see, but didn't the map show an S-type wave? Is that the stage coach road or a snake in the brook? Those would be the most logical to me as major landmarks."

"Aw, I have no idea." River squinted as he held the map

closer. He kept looking up and around the area, over his shoulder, then back at the map. "I'm not sure if this is right at all or if we're even going in the right direction. See this part here that I mentioned before? It looks like boulders maybe or small cliffs even. Look around. These small wavy lines here might even be a waterfall. It can't be the boulders where we found Flash and the little falls there because there are tons of rocks and none really stand out above the rest. These are distinct and big, whatever they are. Where on earth is that? I didn't see that or squiggles of any kind. We should be seeing some of these markers by now if this is the right way. What if the X is closer to the cave and not this far out?"

I leaned in for a closer look. "Yeah, I don't know. I'm clueless. I already gave my best guess, sorry."

He bit his lip, looking like he was contemplating a plan. "Okay." He folded the map and tucked it in his back pocket. It hung out like a smudged, lumpy tail. "Let's keep walking this way for a while and see if we can find any of the landmarks. Look for these four Chocolate Cheerios things."

"If that wavy line on top is the stagecoach road, maybe they're wagon wheels or something that's no longer there. I mean, they are distinct circles."

"You are brilliant, Kat! I bet that's what they could be, if the treasure is really that old. I'm not seeing anything stand-outish this way that would be worthy of being placed on a map. No circles. No S wave. No big, lumpy things next to a tall … *tree* I'm guessing. Are you?"

"Nope. And as far as the tree beside the lumps, it could've been chopped down by now or struck by lightning. I'm not so sure we can depend on that."

"That's very true."

"The brook runs down the mountain and through the valley a long way in both directions," I said. "How far should we go? Maybe our path is not so close to the brook." I looked up the hill then back at him. "I can't be gone too long, and I sure don't want to lie to my mother, who will wonder where I was the whole day. What time is it?"

River took out his cell phone. "I don't think we've been gone more than an hour or two." But he frowned. "Or maybe not. Crud. It's almost two already? How on earth did that happen? The day has been gobbled up."

"Wow. I know. Time flew by. Okay, River. Let's just follow the brook for a half hour more, and if we don't find the right place, we'll head home and come back another time. We can be more prepared and bring real shovels in case we have to dig deep. Now that I have a backpack, I can carry the box and the map home and hide it somewhere. I don't want you to take it because your dog could eat it and it's too special."

"Agree," said River. "But we can still start our search at the cave next time. I'm pretty sure the map starts us there. It has to. That's where the tin box was buried."

"Right. Sounds perfect to me."

River and I traipsed around, but we saw absolutely nothing that looked like the circles, the wave or the three isolated, big masses. We didn't spot any boulders or cliffs that those might signify. In fact, it was mostly flattening out into a long span of trees that were pretty close together on either side of the brook. All I could see now, looking ahead, were brown trunks. The canopy of leaves above us shrouded out a lot of the sunlight as we moved deeper into the thick. "This can't be right at all, River," I said with a cringe. Cool air snaked down my back with a bead of sweat and I shivered. The brook looked like it traveled right through a tunnel of evil, gnarled entanglements. Creepy. "Bet the deer love this dense woodland. Me? Not so much. The only thing that could possibly be buried out here is bones, which I definitely don't want to find. We're on a treasure hunt. No way do I want to get sucked into some murder mystery."

He laughed.

"I'm deadly serious. And none of this looks like the drawings on the map."

"Yeah, you're right. I feel discouraged. We came all this way, and it's not even right. I have no clue how we're going to be able to read this map any better. We'll need to think about it. Maybe the W doesn't mean west or we missed something major from our starting point."

"We definitely missed something," I said with a groan. "We totally bite at deep searching."

"I think we'll get on the right track eventually. At least, I hope."

"Me too."

River and I turned around with big sighs and headed back towards the mountain. When we got to a more open spot along the brook, we stopped and sat down on rocks to take a breather. We ate our snacks and drank some water.

On our way back, we continued to make boisterous noises, he with his clackers, and me with my low-pitched bell.

We slouched in disappointment as we headed back to my farm. It was just after four o'clock when we got back, which didn't arouse any suspicion, thankfully. My mom was busy with a student lesson. If we'd been gone any longer, like after supper time, I would've been in big, big trouble. I pretty much have free rein in the summer, as long as my chores get done and I'm home by dinner. I sometimes have to cook, which I do tonight, and shepherd's pie is the plan, which takes me a good forty minutes of prep. I'd better get started.

River and I tried to plan our next trek, but as busy as

we were, we were now four days out. He clicked his tongue in his mouth as we flipped through our digital calendars. We had spits and spurts where we'd see each other here and there, but not several hours that coincided where we could do a decent search. "Saturday?" he asked, still looking at his phone.

I groaned. "Mmm, my mom's taking me clothes shopping for school. I still need shoes and a fall coat. We're going to the outlets, so I don't know how long we'll be."

"And I'm going to a festival with my grandfather on Sunday. What about next Monday?"

I gritted my teeth and bounced my heel in frustration because we were running out of time. Why couldn't we have found this map in July? "Err. I guess. That's a full week and our last day before school. It'll have to be then. There's no way I'd be able to stand to wait longer than that. But it's very important that I be back no later than 2:30. I absolutely have to be at my Angels Club meeting at 3. We have so much to do. We have a packed fall schedule."

"My parents might be doing a barbeque, so me too."

"Okay. Monday it is then," I said.

"We'll each bring a shovel, and we can start in the morning and make sure we're back in time for your meeting. No biggie."

"Yeah, Perfect." But this felt like a very, very big deal.

"Can you imagine, if we actually find actual treasure, Kat? I might have enough money to buy Flash! I could keep him! I mean, I have a real shot here! How awesome would that be?"

"Very. And I'd have the money to start a rescue program. This is the coolest thing ever." I was about to bust out of my skin in excitement. I couldn't wait to find *our* treasure. I pictured a big chest filled with jewels and gold coins. It was probably much simpler and not nearly as grand, but I just knew it would be amazing! It absolutely had to be ... so our dreams could come true.

6

River

When I arrived at Sunnybrook, three days after my bombed excursion with Kat, I was shocked to learn Cinnamon had already been sold. That was quick. It made me even more frantic to search for the buried treasure. My days with Flash were on borrowed time. It was my only hope to snatch my equine kin spirit.

Cinnamon was a beautiful and kind horse, so it's not surprising she got scoffed up within days.

She was out in the corral, waiting for her pickup, and I went to get Flash so they could at least share one last nuzzle. Even though permanent separation happened all the time in the horse world, it still made me sad, knowing they'd be torn apart forever. Just at that, I teared up and coughed at the salt burn in my throat and eyes.

I put Flash's halter on and led him out of the barn and up to the corral. They whinnied to one another. His mama eagerly trotted up to the fence, in that way horses do when they're excited to see anyone they loved. She bent down and met her baby face-to-face. They stroked heads together and Cinnamon's lips flopped and fluttered as she mouthed his nose and ears. I let them spend a few more tender-hearted minutes together, but it was time to pony up Flash with Angel.

Flash wanted to stay at first, but when he heard and saw Kat, Jacinda, Emily, and the McKinleys going into the arena, he turned entirely around and practically said, "That way," with his whinny and head shake. He was anxious to see what they were up to.

Emily told me she was really excited about ponying because she'd been reading up about it.

He's been doing great on lead, and I was anxious to move Flash forward with the next step in his training. I led him into the arena and handed his lead line to Kat. Now, I just needed to get Angel, so we could get started.

Angel was solid, patient and well-trained. She had an uncanny way of staying steady and quiet, even when everything was in chaos. Even Tom, the farrier, loved her calmness. One windy day when he was trimming Angel's hooves, a huge, blue tarp covering a stack of wood flew loose, swirled around in the wind, and landed right in front of her feet. The large, crinkly thing would've frightened any horse and perhaps made it bolt. Angel, though, pulled back ever so slightly from her crossties but stood steady. Horses are known to spook at flying objects, especially objects above them, and a tarp, dancing in the air and landing in front of them, would cause any well-mannered horse to shy. But Angel was totally chill. She sniffed it in curiosity, then pawed it with her front hoof until Mrs. M took it away. It was probably due to her good training she received in the circus. She likely had things flying overhead all the time. When I spoke to Tom, he told me he always talks up Angel at other farms. Because of that one incident, Angel now has a reputation at other barns, and she's so famous for her sweetness and her story. People drive from out of state just to meet her.

Angel's become the star of the therapeutic riding program. The gorgeous Curly was loved by everyone, and because so many kids wanted a turn riding her, Mrs. M had to work out a sign-up schedule to be fair. Mrs. M agreed totally with Kat and me that Angel was the perfect horse to teach Flash how to pony.

I've been eager to learn everything I can about horses, and I study everything intently. Just from watching other trainers and riders, I've acquired on-the job insight into what it takes to be a horseman. My grandfather couldn't be happier with my passion. He loves horses too. He'd love it if we had Flash running around on our farm that currently only has two cats, ducks, chickens, and my dog ruling the roost. But, that won't happen, unless I find real treasure of course.

Jacinda already had Angel tacked and ready for me at the crossties. I adjusted my stirrups and I was ready to go. I unclipped her, then led her by the reins into the indoor arena where everyone was waiting. I could already hear chatty Emily cheering and I smiled at her enthusiasm.

"Here comes River and Angel," she yelled. "I'm so excited." She leaned forward on her crutches and craned her neck to see. "Hi, River!" She waved her hand like a flower in the wind.

I winked and waved at her.

Mr. and Mrs. M waved as I walked Angel to the center to meet with Flash, Kat and Jacinda.

Jacinda took Angel's reins from me and stroked her sweet horse's head.

I rubbed Flash's nose and scratched under his chin. He nickered in response. He's now friends with Angel because I've been turning them out together. Flash has always been standoffish, jumping around like a bunny, but his curiosity got the better of him, and he's been grazing and playing closer to Angel, trying to get her attention like a little pest brother.

She's never amused but isn't bothered by it either.

I took his lead line and led him around the arena so he could feel comfortable in the space again. Very curious, he liked to check everything out. People, horses, places. He was ready to go for whatever this was, dancing beside me, his body rippling with excitement.

Although he'd been in the arena many times with Kat and me, I knew he could tell something different was going to happen today. He seemed pretty stoked about it. He reminded me of those peppy Jack Russell Terriers before a race. That was my boy, full of energy and delight when faced with something new.

Jacinda stood next to Angel, holding her reins. I walked Flash over to Angel and Jacinda took the lead line from me and handed me the reins. I stepped to the side of the mare to mount. I put one foot in the stirrup and swung myself up and onto the saddle in one smooth motion.

Flash was still pretty bouncy. Kat stood beside Jacinda, stroking Flash's neck and speaking softly to him to calm him down. "Okay, boy. Today's the big day. Calm down. You can do this."

"Are you ready to go?" called Mrs. M.

"Yes, all set," I called back, as I reached for the long cotton line clipped to Flash's halter that Kat was holding. Holding both Angel's reins and Flash's lead line, I said, "Okay, Flash, ready to show off?" My heart was pounding from my excitement. I just knew Flash could nail this and get it right. "Walk on, Angel." I squeezed my legs to give Angel the cue to walk, gave a cluck, and the horses moved out. Using the lead line, I kept Flash by Angel's side.

Emily clapped her hands with excitement and Jacinda walked back to watch with her and Posh, who'd just come into the arena.

I kept the walk slow and easy and I could hear the girls chatting.

Posh also really liked the frisky colt. All of us were there when Flash was born, so we're all kind of attached. "What does ponying do for a horse, Jacinda?" she asked.

Before Jacinda could answer, Emily chimed in. "Ponying a young horse teaches it how to walk beside another horse and feel what it's like to have a human riding above it. It will help get him in sync with a rider, even though he's not actually being ridden. For a young horse, especially a spirited one like Flash, ponying is an important step in training."

"Wow, Em," Jacinda said. "You really do know your stuff."

"Yup, and I'm learning more every day."

"I remember when you were terrified to get on one," Jacinda teased.

"True, I was at first. But when I finally got used to being up there in a saddle, I felt like I was flying. I was up high and I didn't need my legs to walk. The horse carried me. When I'm on a horse, no one can even tell I have a disability."

"Is that how most of the kids feel who can't walk at all or that well?" Posh asked.

"I think so," Emily replied after a minute. "When kids who are in wheelchairs are up on a horse, they can look down at people, but when they're in a wheelchair, they're always looking up, hoping to be seen. There's no way people can miss you if you're on a horse."

"Emily, you are so smart," Jacinda said, giving her a quick hug.

"Yeah, sometimes, I guess, but I still have a lot to learn. I don't know as much as you and Kat that's for sure."

I waved to them from my perch and they waved back.

"Angel looks so amazing," Emily cried.

"You're a natural," Mr. M exclaimed with his hand cupped around his mouth so his sound would carry. "You're so calm."

"Thanks, Mr. M," I said. Without the arena packed with noise and everyone quietly watching me, I could just about hear their breaths, but I was super in sync with Angel at the moment. Flash stayed steady with us and in the proper place for walking, so I think he was ready to move up to a quicker gait.

I heard Mr. M say to his wife, "A calm, steady mindset for horses is a beautiful thing to watch."

"I agree," said Mrs. M. I'm sure she kept her eyes riveted on us the whole time to make sure Flash didn't get stressed out.

But, after that, my concentration was all on the horses. I wanted to prove that Flash was a quick learner and would eventually grow into a fine, dependable horse. Even though Flash could be a handful, I loved the challenge. Flash was just the type of horse I loved to ride.

Flash was a little tense as I picked up the pace, and I knew he didn't quite know what was expected. Angel was quiet and forgiving. I was worried when he bumped into her several times, but there was no misstep from Angel. She'd give a gentle nudge with her nose and he'd get back to position beside her. I continued to bring them around the side of the arena at a faster walk. Once Flash knew enough to stay out of Angel's way, his steps got in unison with hers. I waited a few seconds and moved Angel into a trot. Flash was not a fan. He kicked out his heels and suddenly showed his frisky side. "Steady, boy," I said, clenching my jaw in tension. I held onto the lead and Angel continued at a steady trot, not seemingly bothered by the jittery colt beside her.

With Angel remaining calmer than a clam after the buck-wild jolt, Flash eventually moved into a perfect trot beside her, which eased the tightness gripping my shoulders. I was worried there for a sec that he wouldn't stand for this nonsense, but he quickly settled into the lesson.

Kat, Jacinda, Emily and Posh cheered from the sideline.

"Go, Flash," Em yelled.

"Good boy, Flash!" Kat yelled, giving the colt her utmost encouragement.

I continued the trot and made another loop around the indoor arena. I saw Mr. and Mrs. M smiling wide as we passed them in a beautifully synced trot.

I peeked down at my prize. The brown and white paint colt pranced proudly, and I could tell he was glad to expel some energy in a positive way. You could hear each of his hooves hit the ground in cadence with Angel's. His young, muscular body gave a hint at the solid horse he'd become, which sadly, I wouldn't get to see, unless I actually found the treasure. Since Angel was a gaited horse, her trot was smooth and graceful. Flash even adopted her smoothness and chill attitude, maintaining a calm demeanor. He never tried to break out of the rhythm or teaming. The pleasant beat was probably as hypnotic and soothing for him as it was for me.

Mrs. M. kept remarking how gorgeous he was every time I passed, which made me smile. "He should bring in a good price," she said. That did not make me smile. It cut into my heart, but I needed to concentrate on my job and not on their conversation that was so bitingly true.

I choked down a building sob, ignoring the inevitable.

I moved Angel into a canter and Flash took a little while to realign because he was used to the other beat. He soon picked it up and I was so proud of him that I wanted to hug him right there. This was definitely a success. With a few more sessions, he should really get the hang of this and be well on his way to being an excellent, well-trained, riding horse.

I just wished with all my might that he could be *my* riding horse.

7

Kat

On Dig Day, River and I headed for the woods, bouncing with laughter and clatter. We were much more prepared than last time with camping shovels that folded up in our packs, the map, a compass, the noisemakers, and everything else we needed for a successful treasure hunt.

The ground was dry now, so going down the mountain was as easy as it had been all summer long. We were at the cave in no time. It would be our starting point and we were ready to trek. I whipped out the map and we stared at it. "Hmm. Maybe east?" I said. "We tried west. Maybe the W really does mean water."

River shrugged, looking west, then east. "Sure. Maybe. Why not. The brook and stage coach road run both ways, and we've already traveled quite a bit west. I can't imagine the treasure being beyond the denser forest. We'll just have to keep a look out for bear tracks because the lower caves are this way."

"Sure. Way to kill my excitement, River. You just *had* to mention bears." I shuddered, but I was determined to find treasure and not chicken out. We both needed money for different reasons. I felt safe with River, that he could get us out of a jam if we ran into trouble of the two-hundred-pound kind. "Okay. Let's hit it. Be sure to make noise though. I'm not even kidding."

He didn't laugh as he pulled out his sticks, but he didn't look worried either, which eased my mind. He already gave me the most important rule when confronting a bear: *Don't run.*

It must be hard with a growling beast in front of your face to stick your boots to the ground, but I sure as bat babies didn't wanna find out.

He banged his sticks and I rang my bell as loudly as I could as we headed northeast along the brook.

I cringed when we passed one of the painted-red t-posts my dad put up, which were imbedded in cement in the ground. Veering past my own lands always made me nervous, and sure enough, a chill slithered down my back, making my whole torso shake and shimmy. I was keeping perfect pace with River, and every now and then he'd yank my braids. He had his hair in a ponytail so I yanked back. We laughed and kept going, making as much boisterous noise as we could so we wouldn't catch any black bears off guard.

Hearing a rustle at my side, I froze and turned my head. I saw bunny ears sticking up from behind twin rocks. Its little nose twitched as it watched us. I smiled, not really watching my step.

But neither was River I realized because a hard thud near my feet jerked my gaze down.

I screamed when I saw my frenemy, lying lifeless on the ground. "River," I cried. I stooped and covered my mouth when I saw blood on the rock his head had hit. Tears filled my eyes. "Oh my goodness! River! Oh no. Wake up, please!" My body trembled as tears fell from my eyes. "River. Come on. Don't do this to me. I don't know what to do. Um, um, um…" I looked all around and cried for help, but no one was in sight. It was totally up to me to help him. I had my phone, but I wasn't sure how to tell anyone our exact location. I tapped his shoulder, hoping he'd rouse, but he didn't wake up or budge, which made me freak out. "River, wake uuuup!"

Because of the sound of my own shattered voice, at first, I dismissed the whoosh-grunt behind me, but when it carried again, I peered over my shoulder, out of annoyance more than anything. I almost lost my socks and shorts when I saw a bear about twenty feet away.

A deadly, claw-gashing bear on a rock in the brook! My pulse ricocheted in frantic madness like a pinball and my mouth went Sahara-dry from my sharp intake of breath. He looked at me looking at him, and I inched up on the most wobbly legs on the planet and screamed at the top of my lungs. "Oh my word! River, River. Wake up. Wake up. A bear, a bear, a bear." My gut instinct was to bolt like mad, but I couldn't leave River, and plus, he made me promise to never, ever run. Bears can outrun you, and it can trigger its predatory instincts, so he said to be as big and scary as you can if it challenges. Me, big? Ha, that's laughable. It was just standing there, looking at me like I was interrupting his lunchtime fishing expedition. I kind of was. It lifted its head and let out a lazy roar, maybe to warn me off. It loped off the rock and lumbered towards me with a look of curiosity more than anger or upset. "Oh my, oh my, oh my. Go away!" I screeched. But still, I didn't want to take a chance and had no interest at all in making friends with a flipping bear.

With River still cheek-down in the dirt, out cold, I did the only thing I could think of to ward the bear off and to save us from being eaten. I leapt up in a flying jumping jack, ringing my bell and shouting in the deepest voice I could manage. "Go away! Get outta here. Go. Leave us alone."

Mr. Bear looked behind its shoulder, then back at me

with wet-snot flying from its nostrils in its gruff exhale. Thank the Lord God Almighty, I mean, seriously, praise you, Jesus, Smokey decided heading northeast for lunch would be better than dealing with a loudmouth, zany nutcase like me. As it was inching back through the brush, with twig crunches and grunts, River moaned.

I crouched beside him. I patted his shoulder. "River, River! Oh my goodness! Are you okay? You're bleeding!"

"What … what happened?" he groaned, reaching for his gashed head. He wiped the blood on his arm and struggled to get up to his knees with a press of his palms.

Keeping my eyes locked on the very big threat, I grabbed his arm to steady him. "Relax for a minute. You tripped and knocked yourself out. You were out cold for a couple minutes. I just saved us from a black bear. I did it! I did it! Can you believe it?"

"What? No way. You did? That's amazing. I knew you could be fierce. Never doubted it for a second."

"Really?" I said, honestly touched.

"Yep."

I let out a couple pent-up hops because I was so uber-excited that I faced down my fear and won! I faced down a bear. Oh yeah! How do ya like me now! And not one from the circus or zoo! A real, scary, ferocious bear. Okay, he was more curious than ferocious, but still, it was a BEAR. And he walked away from me. I deserved a little celebration jig for that victory. "Yeah, look. See?" I pointed downstream where it was still being lazy. "You can still see him sniffing the branches about thirty feet away. I had to do it, River. I couldn't just leave you here or let him maul us. Even though I craved to run, I didn't. I stood up to it and shooed it off with my zany personality and big, fat mouth."

"Good for you, Kat. That's so awesome." River shot up from his knees and stood on shaky legs.

I stood too and helped him to gain his balance with a double clutch on his arm.

"Oh, right. I remember now. That's what I saw. Bear prints. Look! There and there. I was looking at them, trying to guess how old they were, rather than paying attention to my footing. Well, you took care of the danger fine and it looks like we can't go this way anymore. Let's look at the map again."

"River Redstone. No way." I spun and stood toe-to-toe with him, but not face-to-face, and that's when I realized how much he'd grown this summer. He used to be a couple inches taller, but now, he stood a whole head above me. My mom says maybe I'll get a growth spurt like Jacinda, and I sure hope so. I didn't want to be a shrimp forever. At thirteen, I don't have many growing years left. "Are you out of your mind? No! We are not hunting for treasure right now! You need a doctor, like, *stat.* Your head's bleeding, which you well know since blood's on your arm, and you could have a concussion too. This is not something you can dismiss or ignore. It is a very big deal. We can return to this quest some other time."

"But…" He looked back in the direction of the cave. He folded a bandana into a long wrap and tied around his leaking-gore skull. "Look. See? I'm good-to-go."

"No. We are going to the clinic, and that's that."

He crossed his arms and huffed. "All right, all right. You're probably right. But my days with Flash are numbered, and if we don't find that treasure, Kat, or some other way for me to buy him, I don't know what I'll do. I feel so strongly like he's my horse, I even call him my horse, when he's not and I totally know it."

"I know. I know how much you love Flash, but we need to take care of your split-open and possibly broken head first, okay?"

"Yes, ma'am." He saluted me, then sighed and shrugged in surrender.

We climbed back up the mountain with me bracing him a lot, and he did okay.

Once we got back to my house, we called his mom and she picked us up and brought us to the emergency room. Her franticness made us laugh when River seemed perfectly fine to me, other than the gash over a growing, purple egg. He was taken in within thirty minutes, but I waited for ever and ever for him in the waiting room before he came out.

"Oh my goodness! Are you okay?" I cried, launching up from the orange cushioned chair that had been my worry stool for maybe hours.

"No concussion, but I got two stitches." He pointed to the bandage on his head. "I got a CT scan, so that's what the big wait was for. My mom's getting my discharge papers."

I bounced in relief and gave him a quick hug. "Wow. Crazy. I was praying most of the time. I'm glad you're okay. Does your head hurt?"

"Nah. They gave me some jacked-up ibuprofen for the pain. My mom'll run my script over to the pharmacy now."

"Good. Sweet. Do you know what time it is? In the rush to leave, I forgot to snatch my phone."

He whispered, "What did you do with the map?"

"That's what I mean," I whispered back. "I had to…"

Looking at his phone, he said, "Three thirteen."

It hit me like an avalanche and I gasped louder and longer than ever. "Oh no! My Angels Club meeting!" I double-slapped my face. "I totally forgot. Do you think your mom can drop me off at Jacinda's?"

"Yeah, but she'll want to fill my script first. From other times I've gone, the wait has been twenty minutes."

"This is horrible. Jacinda and Tory are gonna kill me."

"You took on a bear and you're worried about them? Nice friends."

"They *are* nice friends," I shot back, defending them. "We just have so much to do and discuss with school starting tomorrow. We have a big project to nail down."

"Project? Like what?" He smirked at me.

"Not your business." I grabbed his phone out of his hand, only to realize I couldn't remember anyone's number because they're all programmed into my contacts. "Do you have Jacinda's number?"

"No. Why would I have her number?"

I frowned as worry smashed into my chest. By the time I got to Jacinda's feeling like the biggest buzzkill on the planet, it was almost 4. My stomach rumbled at the scent of freshly baked chocolate chip cookies and burgers grilling outside.

Her mom had let me in with a friendly, "*Hola*," which I repeated.

I ran into Jacinda's room like a tornado blast. Rats! It was a room full of angry eyes. Even Emily. I don't blame them for being upset. I would be too if the shoe were on the other foot. Or whatever. My mind was mush.

Jacinda said, "Where were you? I called your phone, over and over, and no one picked up? And no one was home."

"I'm sorry, I'm sorry. I was at the E.R. with River. You won't even believe it, but we were in the woods earlier today, and he fell and knocked himself out, and I, little ole me, scared off a bear. Oh yeah! A big, scary, two-hundred-plus-pound bear." I did a butter churn victory dance.

"Oh, wow. You fought a bear?" Emily said, her eyes wide with wonder. She sailed a punch into her palm. "Sweet."

"Yep. A black bear. He was fishing in the brook behind my house."

Posh, Leese and Tia cheered for me, along with Em.

"So awesome!" Leese said. "I would've been scared out of my mind."

"Oh, I was," I said, plopping on Tia's bed to tell the gorier details. "For a minute there, I thought we were dead meat."

"Is River okay?" Posh asked.

"Yeah, he's fine. He has a purple egg on his head and he needed a couple of stitches. You should see the bear."

"Did you knock him on the head with a stick?" Leese asked.

"No. Nothing that dramatic. I just got big and loud."

Tory and Jacinda were clearly not as happy as the others, crossing their arms and scowling.

What on earth! I just faced one of my biggest fears and they're upset?

Tory asked, "What were you doing in the woods with River anyway that was so important that you'd blow us off?"

I gawked and the strain made my throat scratchy. "It … it wasn't like that."

"What was it like then exactly?" Jacinda asked. "Tory's right."

"Were you *kissing* him?" Posh teased all wavy with a big beam on her face.

"No! Definitely not," I yelled. "We were not kissing."

"Then what?" Em asked. "I'm curious too."

The question stopped me cold and my mouth hung open as an answer failed to illuminate in my mind. My light bulb was totally out. What could I say? I couldn't tell them about the treasure. I promised. "Um, we were … we were tracking." I nodded to back myself up. That wasn't a lie, technically, but it sounded so lame.

"Tracking," Tory said, in utter disbelief with a sneer. "I hate the woods, with bugs getting all in my hair. Snakes. BEARS. Plus, the dirt. You blew off our meeting for all that junk just to follow some animal footprints?" Her voice picked up with each word, and by the time she got to footprints, it was a shout. "That's insane."

Everyone in the room was nodding in agreement. I'd lost my fan club. "It … it … I don't know." I really didn't know what to say. I cringed then huffed.

"You know what?" Jacinda said, waving her hands and shaking her head. "Never mind. We don't have time for this. We need to get to work. You're here now. And that's all that matters. Where are we on the bands? What did you find out?" She looked at me with spiked interest in her eyes. Her long, dark brown hair was in a ponytail over her shoulder, and my BFF and favorite *chica* twisted it around her index finger, waiting for my answer.

The same terror I felt when I saw that bear behind me crashed into my soul like the Kool-aid Man blasting through a wall, only there was absolutely nothing "*Oh yeah*" about this. My breath snagged. I looked from face to face because I knew I'd disappoint everyone when I admitted to my big fat pile of nothing. "I, um, didn't have time to look."

"Didn't have time to look? What do you mean? You've had days. Did you have other emergencies?" Jacinda asked, stopping her hair twirl like a sudden freeze had come through.

"No, not exactly. I was just kind of distracted with school starting and all, trying to get my stuff together."

"But ... school starts *tomorrow*," Leese stressed. "And our assembly's in a couple weeks. We need those bracelets to go with our pledge."

"Get real, Kat! Distractions?" Tory said. "Was one of your distractions, *River* by any chance?"

"Um, kind of."

That set fireworks off in the room. Everyone started shouting over each other and looking around in shock.

"But … he's our enemy," Tory yelled above the rest.

"*Competition*," Emily cried, canceling out Tory's slam. "I don't understand. We were doing this whole bullying thing to one-up them I thought. It's not even my school, but I'm still excited about it. It's a good idea. I can give some tips to my friends at Catholic school."

"Yeah, that's what I thought," Tia said. "I wanna give my friends some tips too."

"Got a crush on him or somethin'?" Posh asked. She was determined to set us up, I could tell by the gleam in her eye. Way no!

"No. Nooo. It's not for the reason you think," I cried.

"Explain it then," Jacinda said. "*You're* the one who came into our last meeting all upset about River's Earth Helpers club. *You're* the one who said we need to kick 'em in the teeth with our more-than-equal awesomeness. We came up with a fantastic idea, and you didn't even do our most important task that you volunteered to do. So, what were you doing that was so dang important, that you not only showed up late today but also did not research the wristbands?"

"*I* can research them," Em chirped. "I can start right now. It won't take me long." She immediately got on her laptop and started clicking away. I didn't doubt her skill for one second.

All of a sudden I realized, even though *they* didn't have slack, *I* most certainly did. "We were just … like, tracking. It's something I like to do, all right?"

"But, spending time with River is making you slack off on your responsibilities with us," Jacinda said. "This was really, really important, Kat. Can you understand how we would feel blown off?"

Yep, there is was. *Slack.* And I most definitely have it. Loads of it. "Yes, of course. It was a major goof."

"More than a goof, I'd say," Leese said. "A total dropped ball, if not a kissoff."

"I know. I know. It won't happen again, I swear," I said.

"You're right it won't," Tory said. "It's either River or us."

"Yeah," little Tia cried with a fist pump.

The others nodded.

I gawked in astonishment. "You're making me choose? You can't do that! That's not even right!"

"What's the big deal? Are you even *friends* with River?" Jacinda asked. "I thought you two couldn't stand each other."

"We … *can't.* Usually."

"Okay then." Tory said. "Hanging out with River is making you neglect us. Our job as Angels is really important to the community. You may like to do it, but tracking deer prints does nothing good or beneficial. It's a time waster, especially right now with our busy fall schedule that we're trying to nail down. I cheer with the competition team, but Posh and I are using our skills to help inspire under-privileged kids. I'd be equally upset if you did the same thing watching TV. So, what's it gonna be, Kat? Him or us?"

My heart sank because it was a major, major loss either way, and I knew for sure which way I would land.

8

River

While lightly scratching at my head bandage to attack the itch underneath, I removed the phone from my locker between classes to see if Kat had responded to any of my texts. I just needed a simple, one-word answer. Saturday? Yes or no? I groaned. Nope. Nothing. Aww, why was I even surprised? Man, girls drive me crazy! Especially *this* one.

Phones had to be turned off while school was in progress, unless it was an emergency. Not wanting my lifeline to get confiscated by the principal, I looked over each shoulder, probably looking suspicious, while I waited a few more seconds for a buzz shake.

Colorful but oblivious students swarmed around me, smelling of Axe, hairspray and gum. Bummer. My telepathic plea didn't work. Still got *nothing* except more nothing from Kat. I growled, plopped my no-help-at-all phone back into the front pocket of my backpack and slammed my locker door, which rattled with a clangity-clang. What's the deal? Why on earth was she blowing me off? She knows how important finding the treasure is and what it would mean for me. Her need for money was not as immediate as mine, but still, she loved Flash too … or so I thought. Cinnamon was sold! Doesn't she know how down-to-the-wire we are? Well, at least she'll be helping me pony Flash with Angel later today. I bit my lip in determination. *Can't avoid me then, if we're working together. We are going to resume this quest! We are.*

I turned to head to Earth Science, my absolute favorite class that was already flooding my mind with excitement, even though I'd only had one day of it. Most of the kids were yawning or picking at their binder edges yesterday as Mr. Kyle gave the rundown of the material we'd cover over the next few months, but I was riveted and took notes so I could research ahead of time. I was going to ace every single paper, I just knew it.

My heart stopped and my eyes bugged out when I spotted Kat walking my way. Maybe she *had* read my mind and wanted to talk in person. But when I called her name, she spun without even looking at me and scurried the other way. "Kat," I repeated much louder, drawing the attention of everyone around. I rapped my locker with my knuckles, hurried up to her and caught her arm to spin her around. "Kat! Will Saturday work or not? You haven't called me back or responded to anything at all."

She bit her lip and refused to look in my eyes. She was so weird. Seriously. Like the weirdest girl ever. Why wasn't she as excited as I was to resume our hunt? I'm so sure my Steelers shirt with the peeling paint was way more compelling.

"You wore a dumb, old shirt to school? The new year just started yesterday."

My shirt? That's all she has to say? As long as my hair was out of my face and my jeans weren't filthy or torn too much, I really didn't care how I looked. "It's old, sure, I'll give you that, but it's definitely not dumb. Troy Polamalu signed it, so it's one of my most prized possessions. But I have more important matters to discuss other than my favorite shirt like a very important time sync." I dropped my voice, leaned closer, and said, "So, when can we resume our hunt? The sooner, the better, I say."

She looked me in the eye for the first time. "I'm sorry. No, I ... can't."

"What? What do mean, you can't."

"I mean, we *shouldn't*, right? You got hurt last time. Just look at your broken head. And there was that bear? What if there are more?"

"I won't get hurt. That was a fluke. And you handled the bear like a champ last time. Aren't you feeling more confident, not less?

"Yeah, but, I don't want anything bad to happen. It's not worth it."

I dropped my voice, drew close to her ear and said, "Flash being sold would be bad, real bad. How horrible would it be to have him sold out from under us when we were so close to making our dreams come true? You know how badly I want that horse. I only have $318 to my name, counting all the change I found in the couch cushions. That just won't cut it. "

Walking by, that pageant-perfect girl in the Angels Club smirked at us and said, "Figured. Wooo, kissy, kissy," and blew a kiss and winked at Kat.

I jerked away from her.

"We are *not* kissing," Kat and I both cried, but she'd already turned the corner.

Kat growled and her eyes got wet. "Look. I can't talk to you. Not right now. I just think we're getting our hopes up for nothing. We've looked and looked."

"Not enough."

The bell rang and Kat walked around me with a huge sigh and slump of her shoulders.

"Fine. If you don't wanna go, I'll just do it myself."

She spun on the balls of her feet so fast her blond

ponytail slapped her in the face. She brushed the sting and clingy hair off her strawberry-colored, glossy lips. "No! You can't do that. You can't search without me."

I shrugged with a smile and said, "Good. See ya Saturday then."

"Errr." Her growl of annoyance as she spun back around made me laugh as I went to my class.

When we worked with Flash after school, Kat was all business and didn't want to talk about the treasure hunt.

"I thought you said hunting for treasure was all you could think about," I said, taking the lead line from her while perched on Angel. "Why are you being so weird about it then?"

"I'm not," she insisted with an arm flap of indignation. "I just … don't want anyone to get hurt. It's pretty dangerous."

"No more dangerous than tracking. That's about all we're doing." I clucked and said, "Walk on, Angel." She did but Flash wasn't aware that we started.

I brought Angel to a halt.

Kat stroked Flash's neck when he was busy nipping at the imaginary clover he thought he saw on the ground between his front hooves. He mouthed air and brought his head up with a nose huff and head shake for having to work when he wanted to be munching invisible treats. "It's time to pony up, Flash. Come on. Don't let us down. You nailed this perfectly before. Walk on."

We started again, and Kat stood in front of us, walking backwards with a cookie in her palm. "Cookie, cookie. Look, Flash."

A real treat. Ha! That defeated Flash's stubbornness, and he walked alongside Angel at a steady pace, to get the very real treat in Kat's palm.

Once we circled the arena twice, Kat gave Flash the cookie, scratched him between the ears with her pink-painted nails, and said, "Good boy, Flash. You did it."

Flash remembered what we did before and got in sync with Angel for a second walk around. We easily moved up to a trot and canter and Flash only needed a few seconds to match Angel stride for stride. Their rhythmic beats on the ground made perfect music. Flash was definitely on his way to rocking the horse world.

Kat and I put Angel back in her stall and worked on trailer loading with Flash now that he was piqued to please. Our previous occasions were dismal failures, with him only going up and down the ramp with Cinnamon nearby, but Flash was much more trusting of us now, and the promise of the baby carrot in Kat's hand made the usual daunting process a fairly easy one.

He actually made it all the way in for the first time.

"Yeah! Good boy, Flash," Kat cried. "You're doing so good."

"Awesome job," I said.

Kat gave him the rest of the carrot, clipped him in, hopped down, and we bolted the door for a few minutes. "We'll see. Hopefully he won't freak."

We leaned against the back with our arms and ankles crossed. He was whinnying but not panicking or bucking. We high-fived and opened up the doors.

"Awesome job, Flash." She unclipped him. "Back, Flash. Come on. You can do it! You did awesome in there." We slowly backed him out together, me by his side in case he kicked out his back legs. But he was perfect. We closed up the trailer and complimented him and gave him head scratches all the way back to the barn.

"So, what time should we start Saturday? Like 8-ish?"

Kat shrugged, hanging his halter on the hook. "Yeah, I guess." She stroked his head when he nickered in his stall.

"What happened to your excitement, Kat? We're hunting for treasure in *your* backyard. How many people get to experience such a thrill or adventure? Not many. My head's fine. See?" I pointed to my forehead. "It's just a bandage. Two stitches isn't bad at all."

She sucked her teeth. "It's just ... not such a great idea

as I originally thought. What if it's not even on my parents' property? What if we can't keep it?"

"Let's just find it first and worry about all that stuff later. All right?"

She shrugged again. "Yeah, all right," she groaned unconvincingly. "But … *don't* tell anyone. I mean it. The hunt, all of it, I want it to be just between us."

"Well, yeah, that's what we promised already."

"No, I mean, I don't even want people to know we're like, hanging out even."

"Okay. I get it. You're worried about what you're friends think, like that kissy-kissy girl?"

"I do not!"

"Then what?"

"Err. Never mind! Just don't tell anyone about us wandering through the woods, okay? I've been neglecting my very important Angel responsibilities because I've been so fog-brained by the dazzle of treasure, and they're not happy about it. And I don't blame them. I have this party on Friday that we've been planning for, but it's at the women and children's center, so I shouldn't be out too late. I think 8 will work. See ya Saturday?"

"With shovels," I said with a sneer.

"Yeah, yeah, meathead," she groaned. She waved and started walking towards her house.

Man. Whatever. Girls are the absolute weirdest.

9

Kat

My Angels and I ordered Stand Up Speak Out wristbands at the last meeting—with Emily's very appreciated help because I was the biggest slacker and letdown to my friends ever—and they arrived with our rush-order shipping.

Jacinda brought the box to the party so we could hand some out to the kids at the center.

After decorating the rec hall in festive fall treasures that we handmade, we all leaned in and peered into the big box as Jacinda opened it like it contained the Holy Grail.

Emily clapped and hooted and still managed to grab a baggie first. She tore into the pack of 100 bands and pulled one out. We oohed and aahed as she put it on her wrist. Aside from Tia, she had the thinnest frame, so it was a little big for her tiny wrist, but she didn't care one bit.

"It's so pretty and bright. Look. Aren't you glad we went for the green, blue and white swirl?" She got up on her arm crutches to amble over to Posh, the furthest away. "Check it out, Posh."

"Nice," Posh said. "The perfect suggestion, Em."

"Thanks."

We all dug in, seizing one to put on.

"Yeah, yeah," Leese said. "They do look nice, even with our hoedown attire of plaid shirts, jeans and cowgirl boots." She really wanted to get glow-in-the-dark neon green.

Posh, who's forever changing her hairstyle, had it curly lately, but it was straight and up in a ponytail today, highlighting her Hershey Kiss skin and eyes. After putting on a bracelet, she pulled a red and white bandana out of her pocket and tied it around her hair elastic. Even though Posh made a feminine country bow, the sight of a bandana reminded me of River, and also, our big treasure hunt I honestly couldn't wait to pick up again. I felt bad about blowing him off, but what else was I supposed to do? Err. I can't please everyone. I really don't want to upset my Angels, but I also don't want to miss out on a potentially awesome score that could help River keep Flash.

"The carved-out letters with blue inside look great. Good choice, Emily," I said. We voted on the colors at the last meeting. She really wanted these, and they did look fantastic. They were gender-neutral, so anyone should be okay wearing one.

"So, Tory said you were all kissy-face with River?" Leese said.

"No, I was not. I was just telling him that walking around in the woods was a bad idea when I have more important responsibilities. He was trying to talk me out of my decision."

"Well, glad you set him straight," Jacinda said.

"Yeah," I muttered, followed by a cringe. I let her assume. "Me too." The honest truth would only make everyone upset.

"We do have a lot to do," she continued. "We need to go over what we want to say in the presentation. I was thinking we could each speak for a little bit."

I nodded. "Yeah, I really like that idea."

Leese, Posh and Tory, the only club Angels who attended my school, all agreed.

We put on some country music and when the kids showed up, Posh and Tory taught them how to line dance. Man, I was awful, just dreadful, but Jacinda picked it up really quickly. She was a great dancer, something I never knew about her. Even Tia did better than me.

Emily did pretty good, too, on one crutch. The only thing she couldn't do was spin fast, but she just laughed at herself, finding it hilarious. She never let her cerebral palsy hold her back from anything she wanted to do. My heart broke for her this summer when the zipline place we visited refused to let her swoop down, even with her mom standing right there, begging the Soaring Skies guide. Emily *knew* she could do it. I knew it too. But they took one look at her hobbled walk and scratched her off the list. So sad. I was so proud of her for dancing her heart out now and totally rocking it.

"You're really good, Jacinda," I told her at the drink table when we took a break for homemade fruit punch.

"Thanks. I'm thinking of trying out for the cheer competition squad."

"You are?" I said with utter shock. At first, I thought she was kidding but her beaming smile said she was totally serious. "Why?"

"They need tall, strong people to do the lifts. I'd be really good at that."

I nodded because when she put it that way, I saw that she was absolutely correct on that note. "Oh, yeah, you are so right. You would be. Good for you. Hope you nail it."

"Thanks."

When the party and our cleanup was over, it was a little after nine o'clock and Jacinda's mom brought most of us home in her minivan.

Once I showered and got into my dragonfly summer pajamas in my room, I set my alarm for 6 a.m. so I could finish my barn chores before taking off with River. I beat the clock in my excitement and got up twenty minutes before.

After wolfing down two packs of instant blueberry oatmeal, I tended to Sassy and groomed her at the crossties. She had rolled in mud yesterday and now she was caked with it and last night I was too busy to take care of her. That made me sad and I vowed it would not happen again. I turned Sassy out with Ginger, Angel, Morning Mist, Kerry and Divine. My heart ached at Cinnamon's empty stall. She was so pretty and gentle and was a great mama to Flash and I missed her like crazy. I mucked their stalls as fast as I could and spread out new layers of shavings, then wheeled the manure to the compost field and spread it out with a pitch fork. My mom would take care of the five gelding's stalls and the pony's stall. Miss Carol was scheduled to tackle the small barn holding the boarders and Flash.

I was putting the wheelbarrow and pitchfork away and my stomach jumped in excitement when I saw River coming up the long gravel drive on his bike. It couldn't be 7 yet. Maybe he wanted to see Flash before we headed out. "You're early."

"Is that a problem?" He propped his bike against the side of the big barn and tied his hair back with a rawhide string.

"No, not at all. I'm as ready as I'll ever be."

"Good. Me too," I said.

"What's that? A *smile*? You're psyched about this. Don't lie."

"Okay, okay. Maybe. A tad psyched."

"I knew it! How was your party?"

"Great. Our food came out awesome. I was awful at line dancing, but it was fun anyway."

"I know how to line dance. Maybe I can teach you sometime."

I laughed at the image of him dancing, even though he was probably pretty good. I mean, he did, after all, offer to teach me. That meant he had to be better than good. No guy wants to look like a dork. "Uh, maybe. I guess," I said, not promising anything. I knew I had to keep my time spent with him to a minimum.

He and I double checked to make sure we had the map, a compass, water bottles, noisemakers, bear pepper spray and camping shovels.

We were so ready to hunt! And, hopefully, we would succeed this time and not run into anymore roadblocks, like, I dunno, bears. I loved that I scared one off like a kickbutt ninja. But we might not be so lucky next time. My excitement almost overwhelmed me as we rushed to the edge of the pasture to make our way down the mountain and back to the cave.

This time, the path was a breeze. We knew the easiest way down the mountain by heart. We made noise on the way. At the cave entrance, everything looked the same, but I still had those butterflies of worry in my stomach about possible danger.

"I hope this doesn't get me into trouble, me taking you to the cave. I love working at the farm and I'd hate to lose my volunteer job and getting to ride any horse I want. And what about my boy, Flash? I wouldn't be able to train him or even see him."

"Don't worry. I'll say I was the one who strong-armed you into it."

"Hopefully, they'd believe that." He laughed. "They'd never believe you scared off a bear. You didn't tell 'em, did you?"

"Are you flapjack kidding me? Do you think I'd be here with you if I had? They'd lock me up for life."

I removed the map from my pack and River carefully unfolded it.

"Let's study it better," he said as he fingered the markings. "I wonder if we missed something vital." His eyes furrowed as he thought of something.

"What! What are you thinking?" I studied the map, kneeling next to him.

"I don't know. Direction. Maybe we were right the first time, but off by something."

"Maybe. It looks like we were going in the right direction originally, according to the map."

"What if the upside down U doesn't mean the cave?"

"So, what could the U mean then?" I asked. I couldn't for the life of me think of what else it could be. I took a closer look and blinked.

"I'm not sure."

"Hey, look, River. Right next to it is a faded mark. We didn't see this before. Maybe if we hold it up to the sun we can see it clearer." I ripped it from his hand and held it up to the morning sun that was filtering through the trees over sinking bands of orange and pink.

"Hey. Give it back. You're gonna tear it."

"I will not." I craned my head trying to get a better look.

But then he agreed with me, saying, "Good idea," when he looked up and saw how there was more detail exposed.

"No. Look. See? I was right. It has an arrow by the upside down U and then a 10 S."

"I see it! Cool, Kat. That's what we missed. Okay, let's stand at the cave entrance, turn left and walk ten steps south, and *then* head west." River began walking, compass in hand, and I walked beside him.

We counted ten paces aloud, our voices crackling with glee. I felt we were really on to something. Then, we turned west. This direction led us towards the bottom of the mountain, about forty feet from the brook. "Let's think about this a minute, Kat."

"What?" I stood at his side, scanning the brook and the bank beside it, wondering how far we'd have to walk to find anything resembling the drawings.

"We should get another branch like we did last time, to save our spot." River dragged a branch over.

But I bit my tongue when I spotted one that was straighter. "How about *that* one? I think it would work better." Yeah, it was just a stick, but my competitive nature kicked in again, and I beamed like the sun was rising in my chest when I saw the defeat on his face because I bested him once again. Ha ha, victory.

"Yeah," he said with a shrug. "Guess that'll work."

"What are you talking about? My find is more perfect than yours. Admit it."

"Okay, okay, you rock, Miss Wilderness Queen."

I really liked the sound of that. "Yes, I do," I said with a nod and big grin. "Try to remember that next time, and the fact that I saved you from a bear."

River lifted my branch and dragged it to a place between two small boulders, then stood it up and began twisting it into the muddy soil. It stuck up like a flag staff with no flag.

I stepped in to help, and within a couple minutes we had the limb securely in place.

River kicked the loose mud around the limb and stamped it down with his shoe. "There. That should do it. Let's go."

As if reading my mind, River turned and said, "Kat, I'm glad you're my partner in this search, and I hope we can be friends again."

"We're not *not* friends."

"Oh no? Then what on earth is going on? You blew me off for days. You cutting me off? I hated that."

"You did?" I said in shattered awe, not expecting that at all.

"Yes. You're my bestie. Pretty much." He gave me a quick smile and moved on.

I nodded but felt my face flush. I hoped he really couldn't read my mind and know how happy I was to still be his best friend.

River moved at a fast pace. His legs were much longer than mine, but I did an awesome job of keeping up.

As the sun rose, the morning became hotter and hotter, and even though I was in light clothes, my backpack felt more like it was full of rocks. It left a clammy wet spot on the center of my back.

River glanced back at me. "Let's stop and take a break. I could use some water."

I sighed in relief. I'm glad he could tell I needed to rest for a sec. "Good idea."

"Did we pass any of your dad's posts yet?"

"Nope. We're still on my land."

"Kat, since we can't count on the tree, let's keep checking the bank of the brook from our higher vantage point. We might see something different."

"Good idea. I was just thinking the same thing. We don't even know how far we need to go. It could be a long way." I was starting to doubt we'd ever find the hidden treasure.

"True. But let's concentrate on the rocks like you said and walk closer to the wood line versus the brook. Plus, there are those circle things, whatever they are. Maybe we'll spot them. We can't just give up."

"No, we're not gonna do that. We'll keep going."

After a few minutes to catch a breather and chug some water, we reset our backpacks on our shoulders and began walking again. We stepped over boulders and rocks.

I was following the brook with my gaze and spotted an s-curve. Now that we were up higher, I could see things I didn't notice before. From up here, I could see how the brook had a snaky wind to it. It was gradual, so we didn't spot it down there during our last search, but I could totally see it now. The water also rushed more quickly over rocks where it cascaded into a mini waterfall and moved on. "Stop." I grabbed his arm and my mind was whirling with excitement to think that I might actually have found us a super huge clue in our quest. I pulled out the map and bounced my gaze from the crude drawing to the very definite "s" in the brook. "Stay here!" I cried as I already started booking down the hill.

"Where are you going?" River cried.

I stopped long enough to say, "Stay right there, so we don't lose our spot. I'm just checking something out." I dashed to the bank as fast as I could and peered across to the other side. I saw something rusty in the brush. I could only see the edge, but it was definitely curved and circular and I saw spokes. They're still here! Or at least one, that I could tell, but, I was right! It was a wagon wheel. It's there! And *I, I, I* actually found it! Yippee. I jumped up and down, pumping my fists, and threw myself a party of success. I ran up the hill. "It's there. It's there, River. We totally missed it before. The Cherrio! I didn't see four, but I definitely saw one, which was unmistakably a wagon wheel, plus, the s-curve and the little falls. We are so close. We are so, so close to the X spot, I just know it. From where you are, do you see three lumps in the landscape?

River sat down on a flat rock, and then shot up with a gasp. "These are flat! They're flat! That's why we didn't' see 'em, Kat. One's bigger than the other two. You were right! Get your butt back up here." River removed his water bottle and gulped his drink.

Booking up as fast as I could and hurdling tree limbs, I was out of breath from the obstacle course by the time I reached him. "I've been thinking. What if … the guy who buried the tin box in the cave already dug up the treasure and just put the box back in the cave to fool people into searching for nothing? I hate to think we did all this for nothing."

"Let's just see what we find before we start worrying. We're still on your land. So if there is something, we can claim it and split it 50/50."

"Uh, let's hope it's still there. It just has to be!" I cried as wishful thinking. "What does the map say now?"

Standing in the middle of the three flat rocks. River held the map up to the sun. "I thought it was lines before, but since the other one was ten, this is probably eleven. Pace it out, Kat."

I did, taking what I estimated to be eleven man-sized paces. I turned with a big grin as I stood on the spot and then I jumped up and down.

River dropped to his knees by my feet to brush the branches and leaves away.

"This is so fitting," I laughed. "You worshipping me for my awesomeness."

"Will you just shut up and help me?"

"Fine!" I stooped with him and we pushed the leaves and brush aside. River, suddenly realizing he was still wearing a backpack, chucked it to the ground and removed his camping shovel. I did the same and continued to clear the ground of debris. "Do you think this is the spot?"

"I hope so. Let's just dig all around this area and then we can go deeper if we need to."

After a half-hour of an arm-burning, back-straining dig that had us covered in grime, we came up with nothing.

River stood up, breathing heavy, inspecting the trench we dug. He stretched, bending forward and backward.

I did the same, groaning at the stiffness in all my muscles that were begging me to stop moving altogether. Forget that. Even though this was grueling work, I wasn't about to quit now. Treasure was down there somewhere, and if I had to dig to China to get it, I would.

"Okay." River took a fresh bottle of water from his pack and took in a large swig of the liquid, then passed the bottle to me.

I smiled at his thoughtfulness as I drank.

"Let's survey what we have here, and think about this." He wiped his dirt-covered hands on his jeans, sat down on the ground, and asked me for the map.

Still standing, I leaned over to look at it with him. River once again traced his finger to the point of the boulders. "Do you think we've found the right boulders?" I asked. What if I had been all wrong! As clueless as I was in the woods, I really, really, really wanted to be the winner here, especially against this expert tracker.

"Come on, Kat. How often do you think there'd be three boulders in a row, with one larger than the others, near a snake in the brook, a mini fall and a wagon wheel? To find all this again would be like winning the lottery. The odds are in our favor. We're in the right area but maybe not the exact spot. Or maybe it's deeper down." He was tired, sure, but he actually sounded annoyed at my very sensible question. "Have a little faith."

"I do. Maybe we should dig further away from the rocks and a lot deeper. My paces could've been off. We don't even know what we're looking for, but for sure, I don't think it would be buried too shallow."

"Probably right." River was clearly ready to begin digging again, attacking the dirt, as soon as he stood.

I put the empty bottle in his pack, took a deep breath, and went at the dirt again. I kept digging and digging, and I froze in disbelief when the tip of my shovel hit metal with a 'clank'. The unexpected resistance in the ground shot vibrations and pangs through my arms. River was too busy digging in his area to notice the sound. "Oh my goodness, River," I said quietly, with fear that I might be in a dream. "I think I found it."

River broke the quiet with his loud and boisterous, "You did? No sir!"

"No, really. It's here, it's here," I screeched. I broke up the impacted dirt with my shovel around the object, trying to feel its edges. Scraping away the dirt exposed a decent-sized metal box. It looked like my dad's smaller metal tool box.

We both got on our hands and knees and dug into the loosened dirt as fast as we could.

River dug deeper to get under it. He pushed his shovel beneath the box and tried to lift it up. Seeing the box move, he went to the other corner and wiggled his shovel underneath, continuing to maneuver it around the container. I did the same, helping him out. River, grunting in exertion, pushed his hair from his eyes. His white T-shirt was covered with dirt, and sweat dripped down his forehead and into his eyes. I probably looked just as wrecked, filthy and winded.

My own pulled-back hair was drenched with sweat and loose wet curls that would soon be frizzy clung to my face. My favorite shirt with the picture of a Friesian was covered with dirt and I'd broken two fingernails, but I really didn't care. All that mattered was getting this box out and seeing what was inside. I thirsted to know.

Slowly the box began to break free from the hard-packed dirt. We worked until the box had nothing but air around it. We stood in silence for a moment, just staring down at it and letting out huffs of relief.

We bent and tried to lift it with all our might, but it was a little heavy to hoist. Once we got it out of the ground and up to our knees, it wasn't so bad.

I nearly shouted for joy at the beautiful chinking music inside. It must contain dozens, hundreds, maybe *thousands* of coins. But my heart sank when I saw the letters on the side. "Oh no. Look, River," I pointed to the letters stamped on the lid. "It says Stagecoach Bank. No, no, no. This can't be happening. It's a bank box? Are you kidding me?" I could already hear the sorrow in my voice.

"Kat! This is a bank box. Yes, yes, yes! It really is treasure. Oh my goodness. We're rich! We're rich. Filthy, stinking rich!"

Blinded by gold and silver we hadn't even laid our eyes on yet, he clearly did not see the same big, fat problem that I did. "River. It's a *bank* box."

"Exactly. I already reiterated that," he said, but I could see all he could think about was what was inside the box. "So awesome."

River brushed off the rest of the dirt and began trying to pry open the lid. A keyhole was in the front, but that didn't hold him back. He dragged his knife around the dirt-encrusted cover, trying to break it open. The keyhole was broken but impacted with dirt. He poked it with his knife, loosening it, until it popped the lock.

I twisted my fingers together. I couldn't wait to see what was inside, but the bank stamp on the box could not be good. What if it was stolen? It was buried after all. Or what if the person who buried it ran a stagecoach off the road to get it? What if that's what the wheels on the map were? Only bandits did that. We couldn't keep money if it was stolen, could we? I'm not sure if we can keep this at all, regardless.

River threw his knife on the ground and placed his fingers around the bent metal lid to pull it open. Finally, it gave way, and with another strong yank, it creaked open. For a moment, neither of us spoke or moved or breathed because the contents were simply breathtaking.

Tons and tons of coins, both gold and silver, blinked from the sunlight and twinkled back at us. The coins were accompanied by stacks of large paper bills that didn't look like today's money. There was also what looked like a diamond necklace.

I snatched it and looked at it in awe. The gemstones graduated from the clasp down to the center where there was a giant pendant. It glittered and shone like nothing I'd ever seen in my life. "Oh my word. Is this diamonds? Real diamonds? Maybe it's from a safe deposit box. And what is that? Old cash?"

"I think they're like bank notes," River said. "I learned about them in school. They're dated from 1850 to 1882, so this box was buried no earlier than 1882. All these coins are 1830-1882. We're rich, Kat. We're rich, we're rich."

"But … what if it belongs to this bank? Or this necklace, some person?"

"So what! The owner of the necklace is long dead. I've never heard of this bank. Have you?"

"No, but…" For once, I was speechless.

"So, see? It's not even in existence anymore, I'm sure. Even if this was stolen, it was forever ago. Who'd care?"

"Yeah, maybe you're right. Maybe … we are rich." Could we actually keep this? All this gold? Wow, oh wow. The rush of extravagance slammed into me. He was right. Absolutely right! We *were* rich and we could actually make our dreams come true now.

"We are! And now I can buy Flash!"

This was on my parents' land. It's mine. It's ours. I stood and raised my arms in a cheer.

He stood too and let out a whoop.

"Oh my goodness. We did it! We did it, River! We're rich! We're rich!" We hugged quickly and clasped arms and danced and yelled at the top of our lungs. "Woo hoo! We're loaded!"

River dropped down and scooped the coins out. "Let's count the coins."

I eagerly made a pile next to him. I started counting dollars in the twenty dollar coins.

After staring at a coin, he pulled his phone from his back pocket and started sliding his finger around.

"What are you doing?" I asked.

"Seeing if there's info about them. Coin collectors probably have sites all over the place, dedicated to coins like this, which are probably rare. They're probably worth way more than $20." Yep, yep. Look. This $20 one is the double eagle coronet head gold. Hold on. 1861. Hmm. I don't know the difference between P and S. But they are, oh my word…" He started breathing faster and clutched his chest. "Kat, Kat, you are not going to believe it. He grabbed a handful of the mixed gold coins. I see at least ten of these here just in this one pile. "At worst, one of these is about two thousand dollars, but most are in the five thousand dollar range, but uncirculated coins can be up to fourteen thousand."

"Fourteen *thousand*," I cried with a thrill, seizing two. "Fourteen?" I just about cried when I checked out the treasure we just dug up. "There's a whole mix of coins here. Most of them are likely extremely rare, and these are all spectacular, like fresh off the minting plates."

We had in our possession varied 175 silver and 289 gold coins. That wasn't even including the bank notes. People probably collected those too. When we finished, we sat back and stared, both too stunned to speak at the Scrooge McDuck piles of coinage before us.

I picked up a bank note. "These say 1,000s. What does that mean? Are you sure they're bank notes and not money?"

"I'm pretty sure. We learned about bank notes last year when we were studying American government."

I was still in disbelief as we sat cross-legged on the ground with treasure stacked around us.

"Are they worth any money now?" I asked, wanting to hear more about bank notes.

"I don't know, although our teacher said that some collectors pay a lot of money for the rarer ones." He turned the bill over and looked at it, and then turned it up and pointed to a date on the bottom corner. "See, right here. It looks like the date of the note." I leaned closer to get a better look. "It says 1880. Wasn't that around the time that stagecoaches were running around here?"

"I'm not sure. I don't know how long they ran." Curious, I picked up one of the bills and looked at another date. "This bill has the same date." I put it down and picked up some more. "1852 on this one. 1860."

"I remember our teacher saying that the first bank of the United States was in the 1800's. Back then, people didn't want to keep gold or silver in their homes. They were afraid they would be robbed, so they brought their gold or silver to a bank and it was kept in the bank's vaults. The banks gave the owners a note with the name of the bank stamped on it, and it represented the amount of gold or silver they deposited. Then, we had no printed money, just bank, and later, Federal Reserve notes."

"This is so old, maybe we really can take ownership of it." A wave of relief washed through me, as I began to feel more possessive of these contents. I did not want to give up this treasure. No way. Even if River and I had merely found a fistful of these coins, it would make us rich. But this was a whole lot more than a fistful. It was a goldmine.

River leaned forward and gathered the notes and carefully stacked them. "Help me pick these up," he said, reaching for another note to place into the metal box. "We've got to get going. It will take us longer going back up the mountain carrying this box.

I stood up and picked up some of the coins and handed them to River. "It'll get heavy carrying this all the way back up the mountain. It might be easier, putting the coins in our packs and carrying the lighter box with just the papers and necklace in it."

"Yeah, makes sense," he said. "Sounds like a plan."

I still had butterflies in my stomach. It was hard to believe and jaw-dropping that we found real treasure on Sunnybrook land. My parents will be shocked when I show them. There's no way we can keep the treasure hidden now.

River and I divided up the coins, filling our backpacks, and put all the bank notes back into the metal box.

"River, this is so awesome, the best thing in the world. Now, you can buy Flash, and I can help my parents with the riding programs, and we can take in more rescues, and we can help our clubs do more good deeds. I just hope it's not stolen. The necklace is what freaks me out the most. We really should call the authorities to be sure."

"Are you kidding me? No. No way. They'll confiscate it and claim it doesn't belong to us. But it's *our* money, Kat. We tracked it, found it, and dug it up. We can piece it out gradually, a little at a time with collectors or pawn shops, and roll in the dough. Let's bury this hole before we leave."

"Who cares? Let's just go."

"You always have to leave the earth the way you found it. You don't leave a mess. I can't believe we're rich! There are so many things I want to do."

"But … it might not be ours to keep. We need to do the right thing, River, even if it hurts."

"It'll do a lot more than hurt. It will destroy me, being so close, so close, to having that colt as mine. All I need is, like, two coins, maybe three, and I can buy him, and he'd be mine forever. No one would even know or miss that money." His eyes were getting watery and his voice was cracking.

"Won't our families wonder where we got the money?"

"Yeah, they probably would." River refilled the hole.

"As much as I'd love to roll around in this loot, I can't do that, knowing that it could be and most likely is stolen. How would you like knowing that you got Flash with stolen money?"

"It'd be better than not having him at all. Yeah, I'd get over it."

"Come on. Be serious. That's selfish and wrong. You know we need to do the right thing. Isn't your grandfather always saying to live life fair and right, even if others and circumstances do you wrong?"

His groan turned into a whimper. "But, Kat. We are so … so close. Three coins away."

As we started trekking towards our embedded branch, we were still in debate about what to do.

I heard a man shout behind us, "Hey! I seen what you done! Come back with that treasure! You're on my land. It's mine." I turned and a bearded man with a beer belly was hustling in our direction. He tossed the cigarette from his mouth to the ground.

River yelled, "Hey! You better stomp that out. You could start a fire."

He twisted his old boot on the cigarette butt. His face looked like a snarling Rottweiler as he stormed our way with his fists clenched. "Come back with my money!"

"It is not your land. It's mine! Run, River. Run," I cried, clutching his hand. "Come on."

We both dashed as fast as we could to our stick, and River kicked it over. We veered right back up the mountain. Having gone this way dozens of times, we were nimble and fast and the chasing guy, who kept cursing us out and threatening to hurt us, was unable to keep up. I looked back and he bent over and huffed.

"I'll find you kids. That's *my* money!"

We ran as fast as we could to get away from him.

When we got back to the farm, we were both out of breath and clutching our chests.

River bent and said, "Do you think … do you think, uh, it could've been buried recently? Is that at all possible? Do you think it's his?"

"No way. I don't think so. The shirt is ancient. I think he heard us screaming about being rich, or saw us dancing or covering up the hole."

"Do you know that guy?"

"No. I've never seen him. Maybe he's from the other side of the mountain or brook."

"I've been here many times and I've never seen him either," River said, wiping his wet brow.

"And now he wants to lay claim to our treasure? I don't think so. It's my parents' land. We were not even close the property line markers. Consider our map. It's ancient. It does not look like it was buried anytime recently."

"I know. I didn't really believe he had any cred, but I just wanted to double check. What are we gonna do, Kat?" River said with a huff. "That guy sounded deadly serious."

"Maybe we should turn it in then. And I mean all of it. I don't want for us to get hurt either. The authorities can figure out who it belongs to and award it to the right persons."

"But … Kat. *Flash*."

"I know, River. But this is our only option. We can't hide the money. We can't lie. We can't sell it. I stupidly told that guy where I live. Plus, I've been in the news. He'll figure out exactly who we are, and what if he makes good on his threats to tear us limb from limb until we give him the money? What if he's not kidding? If we don't have the treasure, if we turn it in, then we have nothing for him to take back like he swore he would."

"Yeah, I guess you're right," he said with a tone of defeat. "Uh, I just hate this."

I put my hand on his shoulder. "I know. I'm so sorry." I was feeling heavier with the weight of having to be honest pressing down on me far more than the stash of coins in my pack. I slid it off my shoulders and rubbed my aching muscles right in between my shoulders and neck. When we reached the porch, I took the box from River, so I could set it on the bench in the mudroom where we put on our shoes, boots and coats.

My dad walked into the kitchen just as we were coming into the mudroom off of it. I let the wooden door crash behind us, and it rattled against the frame for a moment before going still and silent.

River and I took deep breaths. Our near-wheezes said we were both dying of thirst.

"What have you two been up to? Get into a dirt fight?" He grabbed the pitcher of ice tea from the fridge, ice tinkling against the glass. "Want some?" He held it up.

"Yes, please." We nodded like lost souls in the desert. I'm sure River's throat was as caked with dust as mine was. My throat was strained with dryness and irritation.

"Uh, yes!" River said with his hands out for the glass my dad was already filling.

"No fight, Dad. We were digging up treasure," I said.

He handed River a glass and then me, and we both gulped it down with streams pouring down our chins like the slobbery drool of Saint Bernards.

"Oh, like arrowheads and pottery?" my dad said with a smirk.

River set his empty glass down with an, "aaaahh." "No, Mr. M. Not quite." He unzipped his backpack and plunked it on the counter with a heavy thud. "Treasure like *this*."

"Holy moly," my dad said, then he clapped his hand

over his mouth and rubbed it in disbelief. "Sherry! Get out here!"

My mom came into the kitchen from the living room, scowling at his insistence maybe. "What's goin' on? Oh my goodness." She looked us over from head to toe. "What on earth! Where have you two been? You could stand to be hosed off like the horses. You didn't even brush off outside? You're getting dirt on my freshly washed floor. Get." She shooed us, and River and I laughed.

"We were in the woods, Mom, but look what we found."

Her irritation over our dirt prints completely vanished when she spotted what was inside River's bag. She gazed at it, then at us, looking just as shocked as my dad.

We told them how we found an old tin with a map on a shirt and hunted for treasure, but ever-so conveniently left off the cave part, oh, and the bear, and the angry man. "Since it came in this bank box, Mom, do you think it could be stolen? Or that's it's from the stagecoach road? The coins and bank notes are from the late 1800s."

"We were going to keep it," River said. But after my quick, side-eyed glance, he added, "But, of course, we know we can't, not without checking first." As he started unloading his pack and putting everything he had on the counter, my parents stood there, their mouths agape.

And I said, "*And* this is only half of it," and began

emptying my backpack too. We all stared in disbelief at the coins and glittery, diamond necklace.

My mom nodded, but from her expression, it looked like she was trying to convince herself of the right thing to do. "You are absolutely right. We need to call this in."

Having never been in such a position, we didn't know where to start. She called the police and that did the trick. Within ten minutes, three police officers came over, along with Selectwoman Lucy Malloy, who was excited to see the treasure we found in town.

No one she knew or worked with had heard of Stagecoach Bank. But, she said she did some research and discovered the bank was the first regional bank, but it got renamed a few times and it subsumed, or, as she described it to me in simpler terms when I didn't know what that meant, *took in and merged with*, other small banks. Okay, I totally got that. But the Elderbees, Macintyres and Davises, three prominent and affluent families in our region, responsible for the growth and business expansion of our town, were still influential in our community and at the bank. They were extremely excited about our find.

Yeah, I'll bet they are. Okay, maybe not the necklace, but the rest's our treasure. Ours.

But, they'd let us know what they decided. Decided? About what? We found it and dug it up.

River's expression said he was just as annoyed, sad and

dumbfounded as I was. We hoped and prayed they'd say, "You found it, why don't you keep it. It's been ages since we had that money." But, in a flash—oh no, *FLASH*—it was gone. The double loss hit me, and I sniffed as my nose suddenly got runny. It felt like my heart was ripping to pieces in surround-sound.

River clamped down on his bottom lip with his top row of his teeth and let out loud huffs as he tried to contain his wellspring of emotion as they took our shiny, clinking treasure away and left.

I knew his heart was breaking. Maybe it was totally shattered by now. Salty liquid in my eyes beat down the girders of willpower and finally and freely flowed down my cheeks. I couldn't even stand this agony, and all *I* lost were some dreams.

River just lost his very best buddy. I mean, he was still here, but only by a hair.

My mom rubbed my shoulder and I rested my head on her chest and cried harder as sobs became too forceful to hold in.

I cried because this was so gut-wrenchingly awful, to have the treasure we spent days hunting for yanked away like we did something bad and were being punished for it. But mostly, mostly I cried for poor River. My mom's not a hard nose, so I know just three of those coins would've given him enough to buy Flash. Three. And I totally dashed his dream. I hoped and prayed my pressure to do the right thing wouldn't make him hate my guts. I already lost the loot. I didn't want to lose my best friend too.

10

River

So here I was, back in school, and a week had withered away with no word from the ritzy thieves who snatched our treasure. I felt sick about it. Stagecoach Bank didn't exist anymore as the lone entity it once was, so it was clearly *our* money. Finders, keepers, and all that, right? It was a waiting game to see who the rightful owner was. I'm sure the bank will win. I mean, their former name's stamped on the box, so we couldn't really fight against that. But *we* found the map and *we* dug the loot up on Kat's land. No one would even know about it if it hadn't been for our effort.

Our hot discovery even made the news and had collectors drooling in the comment section of every online article, just like I thought it would.

Although our parents hired a lawyer, it was still anyone's guess if we'd ever see any of *our* treasure, especially since it was most likely stolen. It didn't look promising for us.

Everyone was proud of us for doing the honest thing. But 'honest' was a total bum deal for me. All I could think about was Flash and how I was so close to owning him. I couldn't stop the inevitable.

As the days ticked by and he got closer and closer to a sale, I got more and more angry at Kat for making me give up my one chance to get him. If I'd kept just a handful of gold pieces, just a few, no one would've been the wiser, and I would've been able to make my dream come true. Despite my upset, we were still working at the farm together, and she kept sneering at me for being this strange, snippy person I'm normally not. Even though she'd prodded me to do the right thing, I could still see Kat's crumpled face when the authorities took the metal box filled with our hopes and dreams. She was squeezing back the tears, as I was doing, until she could no longer contain them. It wasn't easy for either of us.

Kat and I have plans to pony Flash with MoJoe after school today, just to see how he'd do with a much taller horse. We didn't know if he'd be intimidated by a bigger mass beside him, but I think he'll rock it. He really likes MoJoe, who will frolic in the pasture with him.

With it being so hot last Friday, Kat and I set up a sprinkler before she had to get ready for her party, and Flash's dancing convinced MoJoe to join him in a little kid romp in the firework spray. And I was busy thinking about *that* and laughing under my breath, so I missed the huge guy heading my way until I crashed into his beefy chest.

He pushed me back and cried, "Hey! Watch where you're goin', Pocahontas."

"Pocahontas was a girl," I said, crossing my arms and glaring.

"Aren't *you*?"

"No, I am most certainly not. I'm not classy enough to be a girl. Don't insult the gender."

Confusion filled his face for a second. "My mistake. Headed to a powwow or somethin'? Surprised you don't have feathers to go with your girly braids and tomahawk face, *Freak*, or that you're not on a horse."

I winced at the insult, unsure what to say as a comeback because I did pretty stereotypically love horses, though, not because I was Cherokee but because they totally rocked. A hot poker singed my chest when I spotted Kat peering around a row of lockers at us. Seriously? Of all people, *she* had to see me looking like a weak turd? I was already acting sappy and stupid over Flash. "Forget it, man," I said. "Sorry about the crash." I spun and raced as fast as I could towards my English class before I got another shove and a downpour of words that were far worse.

I sank into a chair in the back row and slid into a slouch of misery. As the teacher spoke about modifiers and squeaked black marker on the board, all I could think about was Kat and how I needed a *brain* modifier. I wouldn't have cared if Greg or Sly had heard that dolt in the hall. But I did care that Kat did. A lot. This whole treasure hunt deal had bonded us. I saw her eyes, so sad and powerless. Was she disappointed when I flopped in standing up for myself? I didn't want to see that look again, that said I talk a good game but can't actually show real strength when push comes to shove. But how can I show strength when I know a Flash-less future is gonna crush me any day now?

I pondered the scene all day and felt like such a wimpy tool.

When I got home, I checked the forecast and a heavy rainstorm was expected tomorrow, so I wanted to pick the ripest veggies.

I set my phone on my bureau and grabbed the wicker basket on the side of my bed, some shears and a knife. I went out, put everything in my food-only wheelbarrow, and set out into the rows. The summer squash and zucchini looked huge and delicious. I licked my lips before

I picked the big ones. They'd grown so much just in two days. You can never find squash this spectacular in the grocery store. They're so puny. My squash, on the other hand, looked award-winning and bright. Local stores have been buying our fruit and veggies too, which helps support the garden. We also have some business donors who give money and a few pickers who volunteer on weekends. About 60% of the food from the garden goes to the Community Cupboard where people can get healthy food for free.

My grandfather was over by the beets, but with the garden almost 80' long, not counting the corn, he was crouched about 50' away. I waved to him and shouted, "*O si ya, e do di*," the Cherokee greeting for 'hello grandfather'.

He said hello back and something about the sun. He was teaching me words, but I still had so much to learn.

I waved like I totally understood and said, "Yeah." I smiled. A lot of the broccoli and cauliflower begged for picking. I cut the stalks free, especially those that looked close to flowering. The scent of earth kicked up as I walked around. All this heavier, bulkier stuff went in the wheelbarrow. Eggplants. Bell peppers. It all looked so good and it made my stomach growl.

I also gathered twelve beautiful red tomatoes and hundreds of string beans and put those in my basket.

I checked out the melons and groaned when I realized I had a good hour of work ahead of me. I brought all my veggies back to the kitchen and went back to the garden with a crate for the melons.

My dog Jack barked like he wanted to play. He grabbed his red ball, ran over and dropped it at my feet.

I rubbed his head vigorously. "Sorry, Jack. I need to work. I'm sorry. We already played Frisbee this morning. But it's work time for me now. Go sit on the porch so I don't accidentally crash into you."

He rolled the ball up to my sneaker with his nose and looked up at me with tongue hanging out in his excitement. Aww. He couldn't be denied when he pulled the ultra-cute card. His floppy ears and adorable brown face stole my heart the second I set eyes on them. "Okay, okay. I hate when you look at me like that, beggar. Here." I tossed it and he scampered to get it and dropped the slimy thing at my foot again. I did it several more times and then insisted that I had to work.

I went inside to wash my hands. He followed me in for my scrub and I left him inside, then got back to my job of picking melons.

It was good so many were ready, but by the time I was finished, my back was killing me.

My grandfather and I built a special box for the back of my bike so I could easily carry and deliver veggies to the

Community Cupboard as needed, and with everything harvesting like mad as the summer ended, it was usually a couple times a day. He would bring in any overflow that I couldn't carry, as well as the eggs and corn, in his van.

Aisha and Devon came over to help me a couple times a week because with my parents working full-time jobs, he and I couldn't do it all alone, even with the extra town folk helping on weekends. Any berries or small veggies had to be packaged, so it was a big job.

I weighed and packaged the green beans in 1-pound green mesh bags and placed them in my bike box, then set the bigger veggies around them, not in any orderly fashion, but as they best fit. And I left the melons for Grandfather.

Before I took off with my colorful stash, I cried, "See ya, *e do di*. I gotta help Kat with Flash. I'll bring these to the Cupboard for now and do another run later." He nodded and waved as I rode past him.

Anxious to get to Sunnybrook, I got to the Cupboard in about five minutes and was greeted by Sister Ruth from Saint Mark's next door. She usually sorted and organized the food people brought in. I put the beans and tomatoes out on their regular tables and left my box with her.

"Thank you, sweetie," she said.

"No prob. I'll be back later to get this."

"See ya then. Have a delightful day."

"You too. I'm sure I will." I was going to be working with Flash. That was always a blast.

When all that was done, it felt like ages later. My muscles were sore and stiff by the time I got to Sunnybrook. Normally I raced up the drive, but today in my exhaustion, I lumbered to get up the long gravel hill. I didn't see anyone. Kat's parents' pickup was gone. The landscape was oddly still. There were no programs scheduled for today, but where were the horses? I didn't see any out. I didn't see any hands either. I patted my back pocket and realized I'd forgotten my cell phone at home. "Kat!" I cried into the expanse of green with no equine munchers. "Hey, Kat! You home?" I set my bike in the grass and my neck tingled like I was in the Twilight Zone. "Hmm." I knocked on the wooden door that rattles and got no response. I shielded my eyes and peered through the door. She wasn't in there.

Turning back to the farm landscape, I cupped my hand around my mouth and shouted, "Kat?" Then, I saw her, coming out of the big barn.

She took one look at me and covered her face with her hands.

I jogged up to her. "Hey. Sorry I've been such a jerk lately. I've just been so sad about losing our treasure to the bank. I really don't think we're gonna get…"

"No, it's not that. I don't … blame you for being upset. I

tried to … I texted you and called you like a million times. Where were you?"

"I know, I know. Sorry I'm late. I got tied up with the garden today. I forgot my phone in my room." I put my hand on her shoulder for a sec. "I'm here. We can work now. It's okay. You didn't get MoJoe tacked yet? Want me to do it?" I looked at the chestnut horse, still in his stall.

"No. I'm sorry." She just broke down and sobbed her heart out, and I had to clear my throat because it felt the strain of compassion and grew brittle and sore as I tried to hold my emotion in. She was really, really upset. This was not just about miscommunication. It was bigger and uglier, and I would probably hate it.

"Are you okay? What's wrong?"

"It's Flash."

My heart jumped and I looked towards his barn. "What's wrong? Is he sick?"

"No. I tried—I tried to call. You're gonna be, oh my gosh, so, so crushed."

"Crushed for what?" Agitation seized my lungs and thrashed me. "Where is he, Kat? Where's my horse? Where *is* he!" I looked around and back at her, and I knew. I knew exactly what would cause this devastation in her. "No, no, no. He was sold? No! Are you kidding me?" I covered my mouth and nostrils with my curled fist and turned shattered sobs into coughs. *I don't believe this,* looped in my brain. *How could this happen!* "No! How? No. This is the most horrible thing ever! I didn't … I didn't even get to say goodbye! I can't believe…" I lost my war with the moisture building in my eyes and tears finally poured onto my index finger. I let go of my face and started pacing and breathing faster. Having fallen into my worst nightmare, my heart pounded so fast that my chest and lungs literally ached. My blood felt like it was liquid fire. I had the sudden urge to punch walls in my frustration and then cry into a pillow from anguish, but neither of those responses was appropriately me.

My breath sounded shredded, coming through my nostrils like a freight train through a needle's eye. I ran my fingers over my head and clutched the back of it, again and again. No, no, this couldn't be happening. It couldn't. I had to be having a bad dream or something, but a hard pinch to my forearm said this was no mere faux nightmare. It was living and true and brutal.

"I tried to tell you and to stop my mom, but she had a short window of opportunity." Kat warbled, "My mom put out some feelers last week. Some lady. She wants him. She's from out of state, but she's an hour away in Scranton for today only, and she's offering a lot of money for him. My mom trailered him to her, and they reached a deal. She just called. I'm so sorry, River. I'm sorry. I'm sorry."

Pain vised my chest like a fist squeezing out the last

drops of lemon juice from a rind. I shook my head in
disbelief. "No, no way, man! This totally sucks. You knew
this was what I feared most and you let it happen?
Unbelievable!"

"It's not my fault!" she cried. She sobbed harder but I
didn't care about her.

I bolted out of the barn before I embarrassed myself or
said something I'd regret. I couldn't believe she didn't
fight harder for my chance to say goodbye to FLASH.
Flash, Flash, Flash. She knew how much I craved to own
that colt. Her mom's soft in the heart and hard pleas from
Kat would've won her over, I know it, but Kat probably
didn't want her mom to lose out on serious money that
could help the program. My soul shattered into a million
pieces when I hopped on my bike. A wave of horror and
grief crashed down on me.

Kat called after me, but I was so choked up, I couldn't
even speak. I tore down the bumpy driveway, and it jarred
my clamped jaw. As soon as my wheels rounded into the
road, the heartbreak was too great to bear and strangled
sobs came crawling out of my throat with grunts and
growls. My shoulders shook like I couldn't shake a cough
as sorrow's thunder ripped through my body. Tears and
snot ran free and I didn't even care. Flash, my favorite
buddy of all time, was gone, totally gone and out of my
reach for ever. And this, *this* was all Kat's fault.

I rode to the river and skipped stones until I stopped acting like the biggest wimp of the century. It wasn't like someone died, yet I felt the same degree of loss. When I chilled out and stopped the flow of tears and ugly sobs, I washed my face with the fresh water, then stood with my arms out and sucked some strength and warm wind into my lungs with deep, cleansing breaths. I didn't feel any less torn apart, but at least the babyish crying now sat in ruins from the jackhammer of my will. I rode home, but took my time. What was the point of rushing?

My grandfather smiled from the back deck. "*O si ya,*" he said, turning. "How was your session?"

I coughed and gritted my teeth as a wail of anguish tried to soar out. I closed my eyes to catch my breath and find the words. I could feel my eyelashes fluttering as I fought to contain the swell of agony within. I took deep breaths. "Flash, my kin spirit, is … gone. Sold."

"By your long face, I could feel your sadness when you were still in the street," he said, mopping his forehead with a red kerchief. He bent down to pick up more of the potatoes that were in his wheelbarrow. "I'm sorry for the loss of your dear friend, River. I wish I could take your pain away. It stabs my chest deeply and sharply. I know you had your heart set on owning the spirited colt, but it was not meant to be. Everything is timing in life's circle."

My voice shook and tears percolated out my eyes. "But

… it hurts so stinkin' much. I love him like a brother. He belongs with me, I know it. I can feel it in my gut."

"What we desire isn't always what's best for us. Just because he has a new home does not mean it wasn't the right course for him. Instead of feeling sad, feel grateful that someone else loves him as much as you and that he's been adopted. It was evidently not part of your life's journey to own this particular colt, but something else in your future will spring up to make you content because you did the honorable thing by turning in the treasure that was most likely stolen. Good deeds are like planted seeds. They do not come up void. They will eventually bear fruit to bless and sustain you, even though it might not be right away. Remember that everything happens for a reason."

"How can you be so sure that something good'll come my way?"

"I've seen it time and again. Maybe this is the Creator's way of giving you more time to work with your club and to feed people in need. If you had the colt at home, it would take time away from your current calling and your future destination."

"And what is my destination then, if not to own horses?" I started helping Grandfather with the potatoes because his wise words were kind of like a smack of sense. It did make me feel better.

"I'm not saying that visions of horses will stop dancing in your head. They're a part of your spirit and are deeply imbedded in your life's blood. Horses will always be a part of you, grandson. You have a big heart to help creatures. Maybe you should concentrate on that, keeping your horse spirit, but choosing to live in the moment with what you've been given until you can fulfill your destiny. Work hard in school, be kind and thoughtful, and you may eventually have a career where you can help others and own some horses and have all your dreams come true. Life moves to its own rhythm. You can't rush timing. Sometimes we have to learn things and suffer first before the clouds can break open to let the sun in."

"Yes, I know. Thanks for the reminder. I just love Flash so much."

He nodded like he got it. "Bonds of friendship last a lifetime, even with separation."

I couldn't even comprehend or stomach a future without Flash right now. This treasure hunt had given me hope and all that got smashed with unfair reality. Flash was gone, now and forever, and I didn't even get to say goodbye. He'll totally forget about me and our bond and my love for him. I teared up. What kind of career would enable me to help people and horses? Maybe I can have a farm like Kat's parents', that does therapy but also rescue.

Grandfather looked around with a sigh of exhaustion.

"How much more of our harvest do we need to deliver to the Community Cupboard today? Are your members coming by to help?"

"No. I told them I was going to be at Sunnybrook. We'll need more help with the harvest though. But, rest up, Grandfather. I'll take care of the rest of today's load."

"Maybe your friend Kat's Angels will help?"

I let out a single scoffing laugh at that. "Yeah, that'll never happen. I'll put some posters up at the Cupboard and the churches. I'm sure we can find the help."

My grandfather picked up the last of the potatoes and dropped them into the crate beside him.

"My Earth Helpers will be here tomorrow and this weekend. We can finish up. I'll plan on Saturday being our big harvest day and put that on the poster. I think, or, I hope, a lot of people in the community will see how fun it can be to help others, if they just put in a little time and effort."

"I agree. The garden is nearly done producing, except for the pumpkins and winter squash. It's time to finish up and then we can till it all under and plant some rye to help fertilize the ground for next year."

"Good thinking." I thanked him, "*Wa do* for all of your help. I never could've done this without you." I felt a little better. A little. He always had a way of putting things in perspective and making me care about my heritage and future. But when I finally crashed onto my pillow at night, flat on my back, with my palms under my head, visions of me and Flash together flooded my mind, and the overwhelming sorrow came rushing back. Tears trickled down into my ears and I sniffed again and again.

Instead of future adventures with the colt that was never really mine, pleasant, poignant memories would have to be good enough.

That, and a few pics on my phone, was all I had of feisty Flash.

11

Kat

Even in my slouch of defeat with my chin over my crossed hands on the corral fence, I had a good view of Sunnybrook Farm. This place was so much less sunny without Flash bopping around the horses to try to get them to play with him. The blaring shout of silence made me tear up. As I watched the four horses grazing in the pasture, hardening clay seemed to fill my lungs and my breaths sounded rough and choppy.

"Are you okay?" Jacinda asked. "Still upset about Flash?"

I turned back to her and wiped my face. "Yeah. Wouldn't you be? I feel so awful for poor River. He didn't even get to say goodbye. Just think about how awful that day was when Angel was going to get taken away for good, and imagine not even getting to say goodbye to her.

That's so unbearable. It would've demolished us. That's where River is right now. He's got to be crushed and is probably mad at me too."

"Why mad at *you*?"

"I don't know, but you know how boys are. They always blame us for everything bad that ever happens."

"That's true." Jacinda mounted her beautiful horse Angel with grace and clucked to prod her into a smooth trot. Angel traveled the perimeter like a sugar glider and came to a halt next to me.

"I feel really bad about yesterday at school too," I said.

"What happened yesterday?"

"Well, I saw this huge guy bullying River, like, insulting him for being Cherokee and for how he looks. I froze in my tracks for a sec, then I hid behind the lockers. I was scared for him, and I didn't know what to do. River saw me there, looking like some lame, wimpy baby who wouldn't stand up for him. How are we, no, how am *I* supposed to be a part of our whole anti-bullying assembly when I can't even practice what I preach? That's so hypocritical. Don't ya think? I sure do." I spun the rubber bracelet on my arm.

She shrugged. "I guess. I'm not sure I would've known what to do either with such a huge guy as the bully, but that's why we can brainstorm. Or, no, no, wait! That's perfect! We can put that into our speech."

"What? Me feeling like a wimpy baby?"

She nodded excitedly. "Yes! Exactly. We don't have to mention River, but we can use what you felt in the moment as an example. That's probably how a lot of people feel, like they're powerless to do anything. But we can brainstorm ideas on what to do, to put power in the hands of students, so the kids in our halls don't feel so helpless and scared. That's what we intended to do, but we can use this to fuel our ideas. Calling it right now, I'm sure Emily and Leese will come up with the best ideas."

"You're probably right." I smiled.

I really, really loved Jacinda. I'm so glad God brought her into my life and that we were such good friends. She always had fab ideas and had the amazing superpower to turn a negative thing around for good with her inner burst of sunshine. "I love that so much. Thanks for making me feel better and for coming up with a cool plan."

Her mouth dropped open as she glanced over her shoulder and she suddenly turned Angel around and brought her to a halt. "Whoa, girl. What on…? Did your parents get a new horse?"

"What? No." With a lack of enthusiasm, I turned to see what she was looking at. That's when I heard that distinct rumble of a diesel truck and a trailer-horse clacking coming up the drive. "Um, um, um. No, not exactly. Oh my goodness. She came? She actually came? Yes, yes, yes."

I jumped up and down with my hands balled together. I was so super psyched but also scared out of my mind. My heart pounded an African beat. This was my dream come true, to take in rescues, finally, but I suddenly felt dizzy as blood rushed from my head.

Um, did I mention I took a call a couple days ago and maybe sorta suggested that my mom had the biggest heart imaginable, and even though this wasn't a rescue farm, per se, (yet, yet, yet), trailering the horse in might win her over? So, yeah, I just might've back-doored this rescue horse in. I hoped. It's a *Thoroughbred*. A young but already retired *race horse*!

"Oh no." Jacinda must've noticed my white face and tighter swallows. "What did you do, Kat? You did this? Are you crazy? Your mom's gonna kill you!"

"She knows I want to take in rescues."

"Yeah, *eventually*. But if she didn't know about this, she's gonna be furious. You'll be grounded 'til Christmas. Maybe next summer!"

"Probably," I said with a nod. "But the well-being of horses makes it worth the risk, don't you think?"

"Mmm, I don't know about that," she groaned with a cringe. She dismounted and jumped down to the dirt with a double thud, lifting up a little cloud of dust.

Angel huffed against her cheek, puffing a section of her hair up with the short burst of breath.

Jacinda had the sides up in a barrette, and she laughed and brushed all the loose strands over her shoulders out of Angel's reach.

Angel turned towards the truck, wanting to see what was going on, so Jacinda led her over so she could hang her curious head over the wooden rail and inspect the new arrival. She scraped her foot and nickered with a head bob in her excitement.

I was excited too. Yippee! My very own project horse!

We exited the corral with the white horse in tow and made our way to the horse trailer in motion.

The truck stopped beside the house.

A thin lady with really short brown hair hopped down from the cab and slammed the door.

I waved furiously, like a lunatic I'm sure, but I couldn't stuff my glee. "Hi, I'm Kat."

She stretched her back for a couple seconds, like she'd had a long drive, and stepped forward with her hand extended. "Hi. *Paulina*. You're the girl I talked to on the phone?"

"Yeah, but I'll have to get my mom. I told you this wasn't a rescue farm, so I'm not sure how she'll react to this, um, new arrival that I so desperately want."

"I drove five hours. I sure hope you guys can take him."

"Yeah, me too. It's Rocky, right? And he's a gelding?"

"Yes."

"Does he have any health concerns? You didn't mention anything over the phone. You just said he was spirited, having just retired from racing."

"Yeah, he's a handful. We have a small farm and just don't have the room or the time that he requires. He needs one-on-one work."

"Oh." I let out a huff as a sliver of worry snaked down my neck. He wasn't frantic in the trailer, and any horse I've ever known has shown impatience to get out at a long stop, so that had to be good news, right? And plus, he could hear our voices, and probably knew this was the final destination. He was simply whinnying, like he was afraid we'd forget him in there. How bad could he be? "Well, we've dealt with difficult horses before. But like I said, I'll have to get my mom's permission first. But you can take him out, so we can get him fed and watered and let him stretch his legs."

I left Jacinda with the lady, and she started asking her questions about Rocky's temperament and history as I went inside and told my mom about him being trailered in. I made a hard sales pitch, prettying it up with *Thoroughbred*. The thing that probably saved me was that mom was still trying to cheer me up about the lost treasure. We've never had a Thoroughbred here! They're lean and strong typically. With the right training, he could become a fantastic dressage horse. I left out the ugly detail that I was the one who put the wheels in motion to get him here.

She let out the longest sigh I'd ever heard come out of her mouth. She tilted her head and glared at me with her arms crossed. "I told you this wasn't a rescue farm, Kat, and that we don't have the time to deal with a horse in need."

"I know, I know," I said. "But, it's just one horse. One. And now, Cinnamon and Flash are gone. I can work with him, I swear. I'll do it. You won't have to worry about anything." I wasn't counting on Flash being gone when I spoke to the lady, but since it had indeed happened, being two horses less kinda worked to my advantage.

"Except the expenses."

"Well, yeah, there is that." A very big and pricey that. I frowned but rubbed my palms together, waiting and hoping for a reply of, "Yes."

She wasn't entirely convinced yet. Of course, she'd have to meet him first. "We'll see, okay? Let's go check out this horse first."

"Okay. Thank you, Mom, for considering it. You know this is my dream."

"I know."

By the time we got there, Paulina had backed the horse out of the trailer. He was bucking and pulling on the lead line for a couple minutes. With some reassurance from the horse deliverer and pats on his beefy chest, he eventually calmed down.

Jacinda gave me a bug-eyed glance to say this was not going to be easy or pleasant at all.

What's a rescue horse if not a creature with some kind of challenge? I have to prove I can do this. And I can, I know it. I scared off a bear for heaven's sake!

My mom and Paulina knocked out some details and I took the lead line. The Thoroughbred was looking at the lovely and super-calm Angel, and I think he wanted to look chill and collected in front of her because his demeanor changed when he was still enough to notice her standing there. Maybe he thought he just arrived in equine heaven because she looked so beautiful and clean and the pastures were rolling and lush.

I checked him out, running my hands along his mass. He didn't mind. He was clean, rugged but lean. His limbs and flanks looked good. They didn't show telltale signs of a too-aggressive regimen or the remnants of injury repair. I worry about racers being pushed too hard. But Paulina said he'd had a short career because he never got up to the desired speed, but he was a good horse, just frisky and stubborn. Yeah, I know all about frisky, stubborn horses. My heart sank when I thought, again, of little Flash. This boy was definitely not starved, but not overweight either. He bent his head down and sniffed my hair when I held his face and looked into his eyes. No cloudiness or anything that looked off. No visible issues that I could see. I fed him a cookie, and he licked my palm after he gobbled it. I could tell he was relieved to be out of the stuffy, confining trailer and in the cool, sunflower breeze.

Rocky and Angel got acquainted. She was shorter than him, and he sniffed her mane. He's probably never seen a curly one before. Angel just stood there, not alarmed at all to be inspected by a strange, new horse. American Curlys tend to be curious, and Angel was no exception, but she was so done with this introduction. Now that she'd seen him up close, she wanted to get back to Tuesday's ride with Jacinda. She liked working in therapy, but she also loved casual days too, especially with her owner, as their bond was growing more and more every day.

She kept bopping Jacinda's head with her mouth, which made Jacinda crack up because she knew exactly what Angel was trying to say just like I did. She was definitely done here.

As much I love the sound of whinnies, when you spend time with horses, you can often get the gist of what they're saying and wanting with their nonverbal language.

"Hi, Rocky. Be good, okay? No bucking. He's calm now, Mom. He looks so hot and thirsty. Can I take him for hay and water while you talk?" When I said water, he was already leading *me* to the big barn and pulling on the line.

"He decided, Mom. We're going. I'll give him the Sunnybrook spa treatment." I laughed and caught up to him and stroked his face.

Jacinda followed after me with Angel and said, "He looks good and healthy, but did you see that bucking when he first came out? What happens when he's not so tired or thirsty? What if you can't control him?"

"I can, I totally can. I know it." I patted his side. "Rocky seems perfect to me. Of course the vet will let us know for sure, but he doesn't seem to have any evident problems."

Jacinda cringed. "Yeah, I guess. He's no Angel though."

"You know, not every horse can be as glorious and perfect as yours," I snapped. "But that doesn't mean they can't or shouldn't be helped!"

She lurched at my abruptness. "Okay. Sorry. I know that."

"Sorry for being so rude. I'm just tired of people doubting me, and not thinking tough horses are worth the trouble. Even if he is trouble, I'll handle it."

"I totally believe you and that you can." She had no jest in her voice. She really meant it.

"Well, Angel wants to finish our ride. I'm gonna hit one of the trails, Kat. See ya."

I smiled and waved as she mounted Angel. "Yeah, see ya. Have fun, Angel!"

I laughed under my breath as she whinnied back

like she knew exactly what I said and was totally answering me.

I walked Rocky to an empty stall and got him some water and hay. Most of the horses were out in the pasture, but the ones in the barn poked their heads out of their stalls and said hello, except Kerry, the bay Morgan. She wanted no part of this weird stranger and backed up in her stall. She shook her head in apparent disgust.

"That's Kerry. She's just shy," I told Rocky with a wave of my hand. "Don't worry. She just needs a little warming up, that's all."

I stayed with him for an hour, just talking and explaining things about this farm. I didn't know how he'd do with the other horses yet, so I brought him into the corral to stretch. He ran the circuit several times, almost making me dizzy. He could see and hear the other horses that were turned out and I didn't know if he was disturbed to see so many or upset because he wasn't out with them, but he kept running along the fence and bucking with loud prattles of complaint.

My nerves tingled and buzzed and I could feel my shoulders tensing up. This was not good at all. "Come on, boy, calm down. You need to make a better impression on my mom. You don't want to freak her out."

When Miss Carol rode Morning Mist around the side of the small barn, he calmed down. Morning Mist wanted to meet him, and Miss Carol let her trot up to the fence. They rubbed faces together, and once again, Rocky was all cool. *Nice save, M&M. Just in time. Yes!* I breathed a sigh of relief when the lady hopped back into her truck and left with that grumbly roar. Rocky was still here, so I took that as super good news. He was staying!

My mom was not happy. The stern expression on her face said it all as she walked over to me. "Well, looks like you got your first project horse, Kat. Be responsible and don't let me down. But I don't want you working with him until I say so. Promise?"

"I won't. I won't. I promise. I'll be awesome. Just wait and see. I can do it."

"I'm putting my trust in you. I've already called the vet. We can't really do much for or with him until we know what's going on with him. How has he been?"

"Um, good, good. Well, he's been a little uncomfortable and antsy without a horse nearby, but I think it's because everything here is so new to him. Thank you, thank you, thank you, Mom, for trusting me. I can do it. I know I can." I jumped up and down.

Miss Carol rode Morning Mist in and Rocky followed all her moves.

"Let's see what he can do, Carol," my mom said. "He does seem most relaxed with the equine company. Can you see if he'll follow your horse?"

Rocky did indeed follow all of Morning Mist's movements, moving from a trot to a canter and down to a walk.

My mom said, "He's definitely active and spirited and not exhibiting any lameness. That's good. Does he seem to be in pain anywhere?"

"No, Ma'am," I said.

She observed us all for a while, then left and came back at suppertime.

Miss Carol left Morning Mist with me and Rocky because every time she tried to ride out, Rocky got verbally and physically upset, and Miss Carol had to leave. She handed me the reins and I circled the outside of the corral. He was so weird, like a Border Collie or a horse herder. Maybe he was the alpha at his old barn.

Rocky followed after her. I dismounted and saw my mom coming back my way. She and I led the horses back to the barn after a long day of ruckus play. I turned out Morning Mist.

My mom wanted to see how he handled grooming, but Rocky did not like being at the crossties for us, not one bit. He was scraping his hoof in irritation and pulling back at the chains. I had to show my mom that I could handle him, and I was flunking big time.

"Shh, it's okay, boy." I fed him some hay in a portable trough to distract him so we could work, and that seemed to do the trick. "See, Mom? It's all good. He just needs to pig out and socialize."

"Yeah, I don't know about that." She sounded leery and doubting. "We'll see. His possessive behavior has me very worried."

"Well, almost every rescue horse has some kind of issue. That's why they're rescues. But I'll find a way to help him. I will."

We continued to groom him together and when we were finished, I put Rocky in a stall, hung up his halter, and set our grooming boxes back in the tack room.

My mom went inside to make fruit pies, and I sat on the cement floor outside Rocky's stall. He spun in circles and bucked, not liking the smaller box after being in the great outdoors, I gathered. When I spoke to him to reassure him, he calmed down, but as soon as I went to leave, he'd pitch a fit.

Maria, one of the farm hands here, brought Morning Mist and Ginger into their stalls.

Rocky calmed down immediately when they joined him in the barn. He hung his head over his stall and nickered a hello. Neither nickered back.

I had to do homework, like put my twenty vocab words into sentences and finish some math problems. I brought it in the barn and sat with Rocky. He didn't seem to like being alone. Maybe because this was a new place. Maybe he hated stalls in general. Maybe he didn't like the smell of this particular barn or its occupants. Or maybe he had abandonment issues, or, something like that. He got better as more and more horses were brought in, and finally settled in.

When I was done with my work, I sighed and scratched his head, as he was still peering over the stall gate, watching me.

"Hi, Rocky. I'm Kat. I love horses so much, and I've grown up around them, having lived here all my life. I don't have siblings, so the horses here have always been like family to me. I didn't even get to say, "Hi," or groom Sassy, my own horse, at all today, because you've tied me up. Not that I'm complaining, mind you, but I'm just saying. I hope you let up a little on this attention thing. You'll probably like Sassy, but she's not in the barn now. She's a little prissy and is certain her poo doesn't stink, but she likes any new horse, so I'm sure you'll be friends in no time." I scratched his head and sighed because every time I tried to leave, he grumbled about it. I kissed the soft top of his nose. "I hope you don't hate me for saying this, but you, Rocky, are going to be big, big trouble for me, I can already tell."

Over the next two days, that ended up being totally true. I had to beg the farm hands and volunteers to spend time with him when I was in school. Rocky did not want to be without a person or other horses, ever. I always had to turn him out and bring him back to the barn with the same horses.

Yesterday, Maria tried to leave with Freedom, our gorgeous black gelding that we got with Angel, and Rocky ran the fence line, trying to see where he'd gone. He did not like having his new friend out of sight. I called Maria on her phone to come back.

The vet said, other than some minor muscle swelling in his back, which massage therapy had already taken care of, his bigger issue was that he was suffering from separation anxiety.

Between his training and short racing career, the three-year-old horse probably never had a day in his life without some kind of companion, either person or horse, and circumstances had him jerked away from his herd. He probably didn't know who would stick around or if he'd get relocated to some sad paddock of isolation.

Some horses can live fine on their own, having a strong bond with their person instead, like Kerry, who I'm sure would be just breezy cool to have all the hay, pasture clover and person-attention to herself. But most equines need at least one friend to horse around with. Like Ginger and Angel, and Sassy and Morning Mist, they usually paired off with particular horses, even when there were many horses on a farm to pick from.

I felt certain that Rocky's destiny must include at least one other horse.

The vet prescribed a low dose of Ace, which is an anxiety medication for horses, but he wanted me to try behavior modification also. Um, behavior modification? Yeah right. I've trained horses, sure, but I've never had to try to keep one from freaking out whenever a riding horse went out on a trail. I was in way over my head with this project horse. There was no way I could do this on my own. I knew exactly the perfect person to help me figure out what this horse needed. He did, after all, help Kerry because she came to us so anti-social and testy. My mom was sad, fearing Kerry wouldn't work out, but River, slowly but surely, turned her around. Now she's so well-behaved, she's used in our program.

But, sadly … no, *heart-crushingly*, River wouldn't even dang talk to me.

12

River

Man, *this heat sucks.* I rubbed my back as I straightened and blinked at the setting sun and its ribbons of pink and orange spanning down behind the tree line. Hot rays from earlier and the heavy work load had my shirt drenched with slimy sweat, which was also dripping down from my hair. My stitches had dissolved yesterday, and I was so glad for that, because the "dead ant" on my healed cut would be itching like crazy right about now. I wiped my sopping brow with my arm and looked at the expanse that I still needed to tackle with an inner '*ugh*'.

My dog Jack hopped and ran around me with a playful bark like he was trying to cheer me on. Yeah right. "Go away, Jack. I'll walk you after dinner. A *short* one though. I'm zapped from all this work."

Although this food was a blessing for sure, my grandfather, the Earth Helpers and I, and a few people from town couldn't keep up with this abundant harvest.

At least it distracted me and left me with no stillness to sit and think about the cutting absence of feisty Flash.

My muscles ached like I'd been beat up. I did get verbally attacked most of the week by that moose at school again, and that was an added mental drain. I didn't know what his deal was or why he singled me out all of a sudden. His trash talk and racial slurs were really getting on my nerves, but I really didn't have time or the passion to deal with it.

My phone buzzed and I groaned. *Kat* ... another text, asking for help with her new rescue horse. Are you kidding me? I couldn't even keep up with my own work, never mind tack on hers too. I bit my tongue and as I surveyed the rest of the field that still sat unpicked. I texted back: *Tell ya what. I need garden pickers for harvest. If you and your Angels come help tomorrow, then I'll help you w/ your horse prob.*

With tomorrow being Saturday, I had high hopes that at least some of them could come. That would make a huge difference and help so much. A few seconds later, I laughed when I saw: *Are you blackmailing me??? I NEED your help.*

And I need YOUR help. It's an exchange, an even back

scratch. Yes or no, Kat? A while passed, and I didn't hear anything. Maybe she was kissing me off or discussing it with the Angels. I hoped, ironing out the details. I really, really did need the help. It took her an hour to send me any word.

OK, I explained our deal. Jacinda can help part of the day – has therapy at 1. The rest can work as long as you need us. What can Em do? She really wants to help and can't stand all day or bend over like that for a long time.

I thought for a few moments and texted: *My mom has an old quilt for outside. Can she sit on a low-to-the-ground dolly cart on the folded quilt and pick string beans that way? With Jacinda's sis or Aisha maybe?*

Hold on. Several minutes later, she wrote back, *YES! She loves that idea! Thanks a bunch! We'll be there. I'll get up early for my barn chores and be there by 6:30, the latest.*

TY. See ya.

Well, at least I had more garden elves lined up for tomorrow. I didn't know if the posters I hung up in town were going to bring in any volunteers or not. It was always better to have more people than you needed.

I brushed the dirt on my hands onto my jeans and hiked the wheelbarrow handles up to push it to my house. My grandfather had done as much as he could today, but he was already inside resting. "Come on, Jack. Let's walk."

I put the produce inside and took Jack on his walk, then washed my hands and got myself a bowl of my Grandfather's steaming chile. While getting a drink of milk, I snuck a handful of cheddar cheese on top and quickly stirred it in before he noticed. He made me laugh in his insistence that we eat food exactly as he made it. At least he was a good cook and wasn't losing his marbles and making disaster meals like my grandmother did before she died.

I sat down at the table with my family and Jack whining for scraps.

"You've got food in your bowl, Jack," my dad snapped before pasting butter on his bread.

With his head slumped, Jack went over to his bowl with a gruff and crunched individual kibbles like he was in pain or we were forcing him to eat bugs. I laughed.

We prayed and I wolfed down two bowls because I was so famished. I didn't even talk to my family much because I was so exhausted. I hit the sack as soon as I finished my shower and woke up with a start from the banging on my window. I peered out and the sun was just starting to push up a golden blanket. It was Kat. I lifted the pane. "What?"

"Come on, River." She waved me to come out.

"For what?"

"Today's picking day, right? You meant today, not next Saturday, right?"

"Oh yeah! The harvest! I overslept! Oh crumbs! I'll be right out. Gimme five."

My mom made breakfast for everyone and we got to work by seven.

I helped Emily get settled in the bean rows and Aisha wanted to pick with her too so she wouldn't be alone.

"So cool, River. Thank you. It's like a stool on wheels!" Emily cried when I brought the dolly over to her in the field. "It's too much of a pain for me to keep getting up and down and I can't bend over and straighten again and again like other people do. With this, I can sit and push myself along on the ground. It's perfect!"

I said, "You're getting more and more mobile. It's great. I've seen that you've started volunteering for therapy. Is that right? If so, that's so exciting."

"Yep." She nodded emphatically, making her tied-back, red curls bounce. "It really is. I've come a long way since last year. I still can't go long distances without my chair, like if I go to the mall or visit a place like Manhattan or Boston, and using crutches a lot makes my shoulders hurt. So, following surgeries, I've worked really, really hard to correct my scissor gait and to build up muscle strength so that I can walk for a short while with no support at all. That was my goal. I'm doing more than anyone thought I ever could and I owe a lot of that to riding therapy. Because of how much good it's done for me, I wanted to

do the same and help others. I begged and assured Mrs. M
I could do it, so she lets me lead horses for kids who need
to go slow or take a lot of stops. It's therapy for me too at
the same time. Isn't that cool?"

"Definitely," I said. "Good for you."

"Yep, it is," Aisha said. "Devon's now riding alone
without side walkers thanks to your encouragement. He
hated horses at first, but you changed his mind, Em. He
won't admit it, but he really likes to ride now and can't
stop talking about Freedom."

"Glad to be of assistance," Emily said.

Aisha watched Emily get situated on her rolling stool,
and they got to work, laughing as they picked beans.

Even with the Angels and my little club helping, as
well as my grandfather and parents, the work load ahead
felt so daunting. It'll take days, I'm sure.

Then, one person I didn't know showed up around 8,
and then three, five minutes later, then six. My posters
worked! Yes! Or maybe the Angels worked some word-of-
mouth magic. Before I knew it, thirty-four people were in
the Community Garden, and we finished gathering every
ripened thing in the whole field before noon. People also
brought trucks so we could cart stuff, not only to our
Community Cupboard but to some pantries in other towns
because we had so much food. We washed and packed up
what needed it and were excited to call it a day.

Everyone was laughing and the mood was high. To celebrate the harvest, my mom made a veggie and noddle stew and eggplant parmesan for everyone to enjoy at lunch.

I felt like I needed a gazillion naps, but Kat didn't let me off the hook on our deal.

13

Kat

The minor swelling on Rocky's back was gone and didn't return, so the vet cleared him for riding. Since my mom's the most experienced rider on the farm, she wanted to ride him before I did. He took the tack without complaining and didn't have any problem at all with being ridden. In fact, he seemed to enjoy it. He perfectly followed all her commands without bucking or balking, and for the first time since he'd been dropped off, he seemed at ease and content.

Miss Carol rode Freedom at the same time and they did a short trail run.

River arrived on his bike, just as they were headed back.

Totally worn out, I puffed my bangs up with my big exhale of relief. I waved to them and shouted to River,

"Come on and see how he's doing. I think my mom'll let me ride him now." When he propped his bike against the barn, I said, "Wow. You look zonked."

"Yeah, I am," he sighed. "But a deal's a deal."

"Oh, of course. You always make good on your promises." I forgot he was only doing this as an "even back scratch", as he put it. Were we even truly friends anymore? Between me wanting to distance myself from him for my club and him being angry at me about Flash and the treasure that we still haven't heard a peep about, I honestly couldn't tell. Everything was blurry and distorted and way awkward between us. "You could've come tomorrow instead. When I said I needed your help, I didn't mean right after the picking. Did everything get delivered?"

He nodded. "Yep."

Rocky and Freedom were brought to a halt in front of us. My mom and Miss Carol handed the reins over to us.

"He did okay, Mom?"

She ran her fingers through her curly blond hair, then slid off the saddle and jumped down to the dirt. "Yep. He handled great the whole time."

"Wanna go for a ride?" I looked at River.

He shrugged. "Yeah, I don't care."

"Can we, Mom?"

"Sure. But don't go too far."

"No, we won't."

"And don't separate, since this horse clearly doesn't like being without at least one friend."

"Thanks."

River and I got our helmets, adjusted the stirrups and mounted the horses.

We were quiet on our ride through the gorgeous woods, with leaves that were just starting to turn bright fall colors. I sniffed the air deeply but it didn't have that sweet fall smell yet of decaying leaves that I loved. However, I did catch a whiff of food grilling in the neighborhood and ripe apples from the grove.

I loved the beat of the twin horse clops in the dirt. Rocky moved in sync with Freedom, so it was like music to my ears, and the graceful movement, like candy to my soul. I'm sure it was the same for River. The sounds of the bubbling brook and the birds singing only added extra layers to nature's song.

"So, what's the biggest issue with your horse?" River asked.

"My *project* horse, you mean. He can't be alone, like, ever. He needs another horse or a person around at all times. The vet said he has separation anxiety."

"And how do you think I can help you with that? I don't know what to do for a horse in that case."

"Yeah, but you helped Kerry."

"Over a long period of time, with lots of patience. She just needed to be more comfortable around different people and horses, and she's cool now."

"But, couldn't you do the same for Rocky?"

He shrugged and shook his head. "I have no idea. I can certainly try, but I think you're way over your head with this one."

"I am not! I can do it."

"If that were true, then why'd you ask me for help?"

"I just … I just …err, ya know what? Never mind. I'll figure it out myself!"

"Look. I will try to help you, but I'm not sure what to do here."

We moved the horses into a canter and circled the pasture. The breeze blew my hair everywhere but the wind felt great on my hot face. Suddenly, Rocky stuttered and stopped to check out the horses that were grazing in the pasture next to us. He recoiled and I quickly circled him to get his concentration. That worked. I rubbed his neck and he calmed down. He wasn't bucking, but I dismounted for my own safety in case he got the urge to haunch up on his back legs.

River got off Freedom so we could lead our horses together back to the corral. "See, Kat? This horse is way more trouble than what we've ever dealt with."

"I know," I admitted with a groan and a cringe. "I hate

that. I only wanted to help horses." I didn't want it to be this way, but I suddenly realized with a landslide smash that my ineptness might actually hurt this horse and hinder its progress. I broke down in tears over that. All I've dreamt of doing for the past year when I first helped Jacinda with Angel was to rescue more horses, and I was just not equipped to help this poor horse. I was a miserable failure.

Rocky led better with us on the ground. At least I got that right, but so much of this was based on his mood at any given time. I hated seeing this horse get so stressed out. It was seriously stressing me out. We came up the other side of the farm by the small barn, and I told River he could go home. We removed the horses' tack and turned them out into the corral. The ride definitely perked Rocky up. He was an athletic and playful horse when he was at ease. He would've gotten along awesome with Flash. Hopefully, he wasn't a lost cause. And I started to believe that when he pulled the stoic horse Freedom, who wasn't exactly the frolicking sort, into a game of tag.

Just as River gave me a sympathetic smile and spun to get his bike, I pointed at the horse trailer coming down the road and then turning up the gravel drive. "River. Look."

He pivoted and said, "Did your mom get a new horse after griping so much to you about taking in one rescue?"

"I don't know." I shook my head. This was a complete shock to me. My stomach dropped. I hoped this wasn't Rocky's ticket out of here. I wanted just a little more time. Maybe, just maybe, I can hit it right and correct his negative behavior. I just needed to find the key.

My mom was not surprised to see this person. She jogged up with a smile on her face. She nodded and by the time we were close enough to hear, the most important thing to fly out of her mouth was the word, "Flash".

River and I froze in place and looked at each other at the same time. Both of our mouths fell open.

"Did she just say what I think she said?" he said to me.

I nodded in disbelief. "Yep, yep, yep."

We both dashed up to get the scoop.

"Is Flash back?" River cried! "Is he?"

Flash whinnied and stomped and scraped his hooves when he heard River's voice.

My mom nodded. "I didn't want to say anything until it was certain, but, yes, he's back."

A man stepped out of the truck cab. "I'm really sorry about this, Sherry. He hasn't worked out at my farm. He's a little too frisky for us. We realized we needed a much calmer horse."

"Yeah, me too. I understand, but it happens. Don't worry. We'll find him another home and make sure he's a perfect fit." She handed him a folded check.

I could feel the buzz of excitement in River and his change in demeanor. It was like the air felt lighter and cleaner.

We ran to the back of the trailer and jumped up and down as the driver pushed the bolt back and opened it up.

"Flash, Flash," River and I both cried.

He lifted his head and let out the cutest nicker ever and looked over his shoulder.

"Hi, boy," River yelled, his voice cracking with emotion.

He was unclipped and he backed out perfectly, just like we taught him.

We kissed and hugged Flash as soon as he was on the ground. He didn't mind the aggressive over-attention either. He clearly had missed us too.

"I love you so much, bud," River said. There were tears in his eyes and he didn't even seem to care. He was just so excited to see Flash again.

I rubbed his head. "Hi, Flash. It's so good to see you." I laughed when he nuzzled my cheek.

"Can we bring him to a paddock, Mom?"

"Sure. Go ahead."

Not having a lead line on hand. I just tugged on his halter and he followed us at a trot to keep up with our jog. After he was fed and watered, he wanted to check out the new horse. Rocky was equally curious, but they were on opposite sides of the fence, so we decided to turn Flash out with him and see what would happen. Once Flash was in the corral, he joined in the chase game, and River and I cracked up watching them run the fence line.

"Awesome, Flash!" River called out.

"Yeah, Flash!" I cried with a clap. "You rock it. We're so glad to have you back."

River gave me a quick hug.

By the look in his eyes, I could tell we were friends again. Moonbeams came out of my smile. We watched the horses play until my mom called us in for dinner.

We went inside to eat melon salad and chicken tacos, but River's eyes were glued to the corral where Flash was still running. I was so glad to have Flash back, especially for River's sake, however, the big fat elephant in the room was that separation for these two was inevitable. But, at least this time, River would get to say goodbye. I'd nail boards over the door before ever letting that happen to him again. I just couldn't deal with River hating me.

While we were eating, the phone rang. According to the caller I.D., it was some bank.

Mom complained about telemarketers calling even on the weekends. But then I remembered that Dudley Ellington Financial was the new name for the Stagecoach Bank. My mom groaned when she looked at the phone, still ringing.

"Mom! Pick up! Pick up! I think it's *the* bank. Maybe they're calling about our treasure!"

She picked up. "Yes, this is she." After a few seconds of her listening, she said, "Oh, really." Her shoulders sank and she sighed. "Oh, okay. That's not what we were expecting, but that should be fine." She motioned for me to get something to write with.

I went to our junk drawer and pulled out a little pad with an apple design in the corner, along with a pen, and slid them to her. I scrunched my nose at her because I was so confused, and she held up her index finger for me to wait.

"And where will this be? And when? Oh, wow. It sounds very elegant and will be appreciated. Thank you so much." She clicked off the phone, but her notes on the pad still didn't make sense to me.

"What! What'd they say? Are we getting any money?"

She tilted her head and her eyes held that look of disappointment. "Now, Kat. Not everything is about money. I'm not really sure. I don't think so. It didn't sound like it. They invited us all, your friends and families too, to a special banquet in your honor."

"A banquet!" River cried, launching up to his feet. "A dumb banquet? Are you kidding me? That's ridiculous! We found probably a million dollars' worth of coins and bank notes, plus, the diamond necklace, which you could probably buy a small island with, and we get a pat on the back and *maybe* a town ribbon *if* they're actually smart enough to think of it? So dumb."

"River," I said with compassion.

"No, no. This is insulting. I'm not sure what I was expecting but it was most definitely not a stupid meal where I have to wear some lame, constricting tie." He mockingly said, "Hey, gee, thanks for finding our long-lost treasure, kids. Here, here is a turkey dinner with some caviar to boot for your trouble. Silence would be better than a stupid party. This stinks."

I nodded because I agreed with everything he was saying. "It does suck rotten eggs, Mom. We hunted and hunted to find this buried stash, so a banquet does come across as a very lame thank you."

"And our friends and family can also share in our misery and see what major losers we are?"

"You are not losers," my mom said. "Let's just hear them out. Maybe they have more information about how the bank box ended up in the ground. Don't you want to know? Aren't you curious?"

I sneered and shrugged. "Yeah, I guess, but it still bites."

"Tell me about it. Like rabid bats," River grumbled. Okay, now he was sounding a lot like me. My snark was rubbing off on him. He sat back down with a loud huff and shoved his food into his mouth like a prisoner that had just been set free. He muttered, "A dumb banquet? Huuhhkk. Unbelievable."

My dad said, "I know it's disappointing, you two, and I don't blame you both for being upset, but you should be proud of yourselves for doing the right thing. We sure are."

"Thanks, Dad. It's just so upsetting to lose the whole lot."

I could hear River murmuring under his breath as he crossed his arms in defiance of this solution from the bank.

My mom's eyes were glossy. I had told her my ideas for the program if the treasure actually became ours. I'm sure she felt disappointed that all her dreams were washed away with one phone call.

River and I cleaned up the kitchen and returned to the barn so we could say goodbye to Flash and Rocky.

We complained some more about the fate of our treasure. There was no way a banquet could compare to having our dreams come true. We wonderfully and unexpectedly just got Flash back, and now, River was back to square one with absolutely no way to buy him.

Over the next few days, I noticed Rocky and Flash were spending a lot of time together, but if Flash got sold again, Rocky might have a relapse in his overall happiness. He was on the anxiety meds, but that was only a Band-aid over a gushing gash. I really needed to get to the bottom of his behavior and find a way to correct it quickly, but I was flunking. Feeling like the biggest screwup on the planet, I took my bowl of cereal to the breakfast bar where my dad was reading the paper and drinking his black coffee. I desperately needed advice.

"Dad, um, I feel like I maybe might've rushed this whole project horse thing. Angel was an easy horse for Jacinda. She behaved like a dream, but Rocky, I hate to say this, is a total beastly nightmare."

"Your mom's told me he's been having trouble with anxiety."

"He improved a lot, like a lot, especially since Flash got back, but it's not enough. Who knows how long Flash'll be here. When he gets sold again, Rocky could and very well might freak out and spiral out of control. Rescuing and training horses is what I've wanted to do for a long time now, but I've realized I totally jumped the gun in getting Rocky here."

"You think your thoughts and prayers brought him here?"

"Well, no. My blabby words over the phone might'a had something more to do with that."

He winked at me. "Yeah, I kinda figured."

"You did?" I said, astonished that he wasn't mad at me since it was one mighty expensive nudge I put out there. "You're not peeved?"

"No, I know how caring you are. Your heart's in the right place."

"Yeah, but a lot of good that did me. So, what do I do now? This horse's problem is too big for me to fix. I'm ready to pull out my hair. My desire to have him here ended up not being what's best for his state of mind, or mine, and now he's suffering because I'm inept and don't know what to do or how to help him. I'm a total failure. Taking care of him is taking up so much time, that I don't have time for anything else. I haven't ridden Sassy in like ten days. I can't straighten my hair because it takes a whopping twenty minutes that I don't have, so now I'm back to being a mop-topped Muppet. My friends are off having fun and helping the community, doing angelic things, and I'm stuck taking care of this one demanding horse. I love him, I do, but it's so, so hard. Jacinda's a cheerleader now, and at this time, I couldn't even dream of doing anything like that. I can't even paint. There's this art contest, right? I saw a poster up at school. The winner can get $5,000! And I don't even have time to paint one picture."

"I can tell you've been stressed. Knowing your limitations is not failure. None of us can do everything we want to do and that's okay. You got yourself into this pit, and you need to find a way out of it. I understand the desire to do such a grownup thing with rescuing horses when you have such a big heart, but now that you're in the thick of it, you have no time to just be a kid."

"Yes, that's it exactly. And no time to breathe."

"Know what I know for sure?"

"What's that?"

"That you can and will find a way to fix it. I know you have the power and brains to come up with a solution that works for everyone. It might take some effort and time, but I fully believe you will sort it all out."

"Wow. Really? That means a lot to me to hear that you have so much confidence in me. Thank you, Daddy. Your kick in the butt really helped."

"Glad to be of service." He clutched my head one-handed, pulled me closer, and kissed my brow. "Love you, Katarina."

"Thanks. Love you too." I still didn't know how to help Rocky, but I dug into my cereal with a lot more confidence. I have been known to rock it. I did, after all, fight off a bear! Oh yeah. If I can do *that*, then I can surely find a way to win for both of our sakes.

River

That muscle-head in school caught up with me again. Man, what's this dude's deal? I huffed when his angry glare rushed my way. I was tired of dealing with him. He could break me in half with his bare hands, and yet he used words as a knife. I think he liked seeing my reaction, and the agony of losing Flash had me too upset to care to fight. Now, I was ready to roar. Bring it on! Gimme your best shot.

He reached behind my head and yanked my ponytail. "Hey, Tonto. I hear you garden. You crochet too? Wow, you gotta be the lamest kid in school."

I stood as tall as I could and looked him in the eye. "No, I *don't* crochet, but you are so right. I *am* lame. I should've thought of that. I give food to the poor. Some blankets would be awesome too. Thanks for the tip, Cowboy." I patted him on the shoulder and walked past his face scrunched with confusion.

"Wait. You're thanking me? I don't get it."

"It was an excellent idea … from someone so brainless." Okay, maybe I could've left off that mean part, but I needed a comeback jab that was legit.

He recoiled and then got up in my face with his fists clenched. He sucked his teeth.

If this dude actually hit me, they had no tolerance here, and there were cameras to prove my case. He'd be out the door so fast. Already, I could report what he's done, but I figure he's just talkin' smack to get his daily kicks. I don't really take it to heart. It's annoying more than anything when I've got more important things to do and worry about. The racist stuff ticks me off though, not so much for me, but my big family of close and distant relatives.

"You callin' me brainless?"

"No, you're calling yourself brainless. Only idiots have to stoop to trashing someone for no good reason."

"Oh, I got…"

"*I've* got," I interrupted. "If you're going to fling a dagger, at least use proper grammar. You just proved my point."

He stammered, his mouth moving like a fish out of water. He looked around, for some backup maybe. When he got none, he left me. "Whatever. You're not worth it."

Hmm. I may be smaller, but I outmatched him in wits, and he knew it.

I carried the thrill of my victory all day, and it gave me confidence that I might actually be able to help Kat with her 'problem' horse. I sure hoped.

When I showed up at the farm after school she was not happy, which, thankfully, had nothing to do with me.

"Can you believe not even one farm out of thirty-two can take Rocky? I spent all afternoon calling people and got nothing but nos."

"I'm sorry. That's a bummer. So what are you going to do now?

She shrugged. "I don't know. But Rocky seems to be doing a lot better with Flash."

"Want me to get him?" I said, pointing at the barn behind me with my thumb.

"Yeah, that'd be awesome. I was just about to. I love watching them play together."

"Me too." I turned and went to get Flash from the barn and spotted Devon running over. I wanted to own Flash more than ever, but didn't know how in the world I could get a deal done.

Devon waved and cried, "Hi, River. Gettin' Flash? I'm so, so glad he's back. Aren't you?"

I rubbed his fuzzy black curls that were cropped close to his head. "More than you can even imagine."

"Is it true you and Kat found treasure?"

"Yeah! Who told you that?"

"Oh, Mrs. M. She invited us to your banquet to celebrate your good deeds."

"Yeah, some good deeds," I muttered in annoyance. I wished my attitude could be better, but I was still bummed and miffed about what felt like a slap in the face from the bank.

My grandfather tried to make me see it in a brighter light. He and my parents were really excited to see me and Kat get the red-carpet treatment. He said this was just the beginning of good things for me. Being recognized and celebrated for honesty was indeed an honor, especially since selfishness was more commonplace today.

"Do I have to wear a tie?" Devon asked with a whine.

"No, *you* don't. But I probably will because I heard there'll be camera crews and stuff."

"Think you'll be on the news?"

"Yeah, that's what I meant."

"Cool. I'll finally know a star." He whipped his hands in the air and bowed.

A *star*, huh? That made me laugh and perked my mood.

In the barn, I handed Devon the halter so he could slide it over Flash's head. He whinnied with excitement to see us. I opened his stall and let Devon lead him out to the round pen to spend time with Rocky.

"You're doin' great on lead, Devon. See? I told you horses weren't so bad."

"Yeah, not bad I guess. But Flash is always cool."

"Always," I agreed with a nod.

Kat was already seeing how Rocky reacted to the lunge whip when we arrived, but he stopped when Devon led Flash over. "Hi, you gonna work Flash? I'm finished with Rocky."

"Yup. Devon, hold the gate open for Kat."

Kat walked Rocky out and I brought Flash into the round pen.

Devon closed the gate, and I began working with Flash.

Aisha had been watching Kat and Rocky with wide-eyed attention and the biggest smile. She clapped and giggled when she led Rocky over to her. She stroked his face. "Yay! Rocky did so good. You're a great trainer, Kat."

Kat sneered at me when Aisha gave the compliment. She was being so hard on herself for not being able to completely break through with Rocky. I could see her straining in her drive to fix him and her frustration at not being able to do it on her own.

"He's following commands well too," I said, trying to pump her up.

"Flash rocks!" Devon said with a fist pump.

"*He's* good too," I said, "but I was really referring to Rocky. We're not sure if he's gonna work out here."

Devon's mouth dropped open and he had tears in his eyes. "But … he has to. I like Rocky. Don't give up on him."

"It's not a matter of giving up!" Kat snapped. "We don't know enough to help him with his separation anxiety. He flips out without people or other horses around."

"Yeah, I know," Devon said. "But sometimes emotional problems just need a steady helper to make them go away. Thinking people will ditch only makes it worse."

"Right. Exactly. Maybe Rocky's scared of that," Kat said with wider eyes like a light bulb turned on in her head. "Hey, River, what if we treat Rocky like a baby? Remember how your cousin Dree had to learn that someone playing peek-a-boo was still there? She'd cry and cry, and the more we showed her that the person hadn't really disappeared, she finally got it and started to enjoy the game and laugh. Maybe we can take Flash out of the pen, for a minute then bring him right back. Then do it again and again. Once Rocky is calm with it, we can make it a little bit longer. Don't you think he'll start to see that Flash is really not gone?"

"Yeah! That's a great idea! It's worth a shot."

Kat and I switched places again, with her and Rocky in the round pen and me outside of it with Flash. I walked Flash around the big barn where he was out of Rocky's view. It sounded like Rocky was freaking out. I peeked and saw him circling the fence line. He wasn't launching up or bucking, but he was distressed. I didn't wait a full minute. I did forty seconds. I didn't want him to rear back and jump the fence to come looking for Flash.

Rocky calmed down when Flash was back within his sight. I did it again and again, and Rocky eventually stopped fussing when Flash left the area.

Devon and Aisha's mom came over to get them as I was leading Flash back to the round pen, and she got sucked into watching too.

"You like horses now, Devon?" his mom said. "That's great."

"Well, *these* guys. They're just like me."

Rocky was excited to see Flash again, but the kids were jumping up and down and celebrating the minor victory. Kat's plan did the trick, at least for one day. We could research some more tips, and if we kept doing things like this, it probably would help him over this hurdle to being a well-trained horse again. But if Flash gets sold, Rocky could have a major setback. That thought circled in my mind and turned my lip corners down. I didn't want to tell Kat what I was thinking because the last thing she needed was a reality check in this moment. I wanted to let her enjoy this small gain she'd made with Rocky's behavior.

Kat walked Aisha and Devon to their van with their mom. They were chattering in excitement the whole way.

I turned out Flash and Rocky and watched them playing and racing in the rolling pasture. They were a lot alike. I prayed whoever bought Flash might consider taking Rocky too. These two could bond like brothers and do so much good for one another.

Man, life rots sometimes. My heart ached thinking about the anguish that will very likely crash into me and poor Rocky once again. He needed a lot of work, yeah, but I could see, clear as day, that he wasn't a bad horse by any means. He was just a little broken inside and needed a friend who wouldn't leave or let him down.

Rocky and Flash didn't complain when I whistled for them to come back. They had a fun and productive day and trotted over. Even though they were charged up from a night of athletics and fun, they went to their stalls easily.

Today's success helped melt a little of my icy disappointment over the banquet. I still found it totally lame, but when I x-ed out the day on the calendar, I was getting a little excited. At least Kat and I would get some props in front of our family and friends. Maybe the exposure would benefit our clubs in some way.

I didn't even complain about my crisp, white shirt and bolo tie, but I did keep my top button undone so I could breathe. At least I felt kinda cool in my cowboy boots.

When my family stepped out to hop into my mom's

car, I was stunned to see a limo in the driveway that was sent to pick us up.

"Did you know about this?" my mom asked my dad.

"No, I had no clue."

"Wow. A limo," I said. "They're going all out. Maybe we'll actually get more than turkey."

My grandfather's face wrinkled at the eyes when he shot me that look he gives me whenever he's challenging me to be grateful for even the smallest of gifts.

I nodded that I got his message and would shut off my stinker mood. Maybe this would be a fun night, but I knew for certain, that if I continued to be sour, it wouldn't be. We were buzzing with excitement when the driver got in and headed the limo down our driveway.

Television cameras were in the parking lot when we arrived. A crowd of well-dressed people waved as the black beauty we were in followed the curved drive. There was indeed a red carpet. I did not expect to be treated like royalty or a movie star. The crowd cheered and clamored for our attention when we stepped out.

"I'm excited," I fibbed a little. "We're so glad to be here."

"Love you, River!" some girl yelled.

Devon was right. I *am* a star. A small-town one with likely less than fifteen minutes of glitter time, but still, it was fun to be adored however briefly.

A man in a tux opened the hotel door for us. And as we walked in through the entry, I looked up to see a shimmering chandelier overhead with a gazillion, dangling crystals. It looked like an upside down, tiered wedding cake but one that sparkled in its own golden light. A burgundy carpet with thousands of diamond shapes held a big, ornate, twelve-point star under the fancy light fixture.

We followed the crowd into what I'm guessing was the biggest banquet room here. It was a packed house. Wow. A lot of people were here to celebrate us.

The tables were decked out like we were at a prince's ball, but everyone was either seated or getting a seat on upholstered chairs that were in rows up by a stage.

I spotted Kat up front. She was in a short-sleeve ruby red, velvet dress with thin white lace trim, and my stomach dropped. I froze.

My mother, clearly not expecting me to stop cold, crashed into my back.

"Sorry," I said. I smiled at Kat when she turned her head as we came in, but I felt like I was sporting a goofy grin. "Am I supposed to sit up there with Kat, Mom? Why are we singled out like we're at a prom?"

Kids from both clubs waved, and I waved back.

"This is to honor you," she said. "The bankers probably want you to feel special."

"Uh, okay." I felt confused more than anything. My legs wobbled when I walked over to join Kat. I couldn't recall ever seeing her in a dress, but she looked totally cute, especially with the sides of her hair braided back into a center ponytail. "Hi."

"Hi. You don't look like yourself," she said, pointing to my outfit.

"Neither do you," I said. "I'm used to seeing you with smudges." *Man. Slap head! You idiot!*

Trust me, I realized my big blunder before she cried, "Smudges! Gosh, you are so rude."

I wanted to say she looked cute either way, but that was ... weird. "Well, it's true. Not that I mind though."

"You don't?"

"Nope. It's kinda cool."

She was staring ahead, but when I turned my head, I saw the sly smile on her lips.

I looked over my shoulder and yanked on my bolo tie. "What's going on here? You know?"

She looked behind her too. "Nope. We're supposed to sit here for the prestigious awards."

"Yipp ... ee," I said with a sarcastic tone that made her laugh. "No," I snapped, correcting myself. "I decided I was going to make the most of this experience and accept whatever is given, even if it's just praise and some turkey."

"Yeah, me too." She leaned closer to my ear and muttered, "Even though it bites."

That made me crack up, but the conversation in the room simmered down at exactly that moment, and that made Kat laugh. I was glad we had matching responses to this hilarity. People sneered, not knowing why we were laughing, and that only made it funnier.

We waved and vowed to be cool, but I still had to fight back snickers.

I wonder how many people here think we deserved the treasure we found instead of it going to the bank.

I turned my attention to the podium, where a man who introduced himself at Morris Elderbee stood and cleared his throat. He was polished and smooth, and his genuine, jovial smile had the ability to make the audience sit back and relax.

"Thank you, everyone, for joining for this celebration. My family was one of three that forged Stagecoach Bank in 1835. We've merged and rebranded since then, but we've never forgotten our loss or the fracture within our community. A robbery occurred in 1882, and it hit my grandmother particularly hard because one of the safe deposit boxes pilfered contained her heirloom diamond necklace. My family offered a reward for its return, as did the bank for the stolen currency, but when Colby Jacobs who committed the crime was killed by gunshot in another bank robbery, all hope was lost that it would ever be found. We stand here today in joyous celebration because of these two persistent teens, who not only searched until they found our stolen money but they did the honest thing and turned it in to its rightful owner. Would you kids please join me on the stage?"

Kat and I both walked up to join him. Dozens of smiles beamed back at us and that warmed my heart.

"If you don't know these two heroes, yes, I'll call them heroes, let me introduce Katarina McKinley and River Redstone. It gives me great pleasure to present these certificates of appreciation to Kat and River."

Certificates of appreciation? Overcome with a tidal wave of disappointment, I curled my lips in to keep from shouting and my shoulders locked so I wouldn't slump.

He continued, "I think, first, I need to tell all of you how tremendously blessed we are to have these two innovative and caring people within our community. Every day, they work to make a difference. Not only did they pursue the hidden treasure, they're known throughout this town for their good deeds."

Applause broke out.

"These two teenagers represent the best of our youth, volunteering at the Therapeutic Riding Program at Sunnybrook Farm."

He shared the benefits of therapy with the audience

and mentioned the annual fundraiser and there was more applause.

"These teens also started their own clubs to help others. Kat is a founding member of Angels Club, which reaches out to spread some kindness and help anyone in need. And River and his friends started a club called Earth Helpers and with his grandfather's direction and advice, planted a community garden at his home farm. Most of the produce is donated to the Community Cupboard."

We got big cheers and shout-outs for that. I couldn't help but smile from the bottom of my heart. A certificate was pretty lame, and I held it limply in my hand, but the glee I could see on everyone's faces made all my heartbreak and disappointment worth it. I felt so loved.

"In addition to the certificates of appreciation, it is our great honor to award Kat and River with the reward money from both my family and the bank."

What? Reward money? I was not expecting money at all. My mouth dropped open wide and I swung my gaze to Kat. She wore the same expression.

Thinking I heard wrong, I looked out to the audience to see if we were on some trick camera show. I caught Mrs. M's squinty-eyed expression first. She had her hands clasped together under her chin. Tears quickly trickled. She looked so proud of us. This was not a joke. If it was, it was a very, very mean one.

Mr. Elderbee continued, "We are very happy to present Kat and River with $75,000 each from Dudley Ellington Financial as a trust for their college education and $200,000 each from my very grateful and ecstatic family. We are thrilled beyond measure to have our precious heirloom back."

Two hundred... Two hundred... I stood there stunned, with my mouth still hanging open.

The cheers that broke out were deafening.

I looked at Kat again and she was equally shocked. I think she was as scared to move or breathe as I was, like we could wake up from a dream.

Camera flashes clicked and the claps kept looping. People got up on their feet.

Kat leaned over and said through a clenched jaw, "Are we really rich? Is this a joke?"

"It'd better not be a joke."

A woman in a pant suit walked on stage and handed us those big presentation checks they give people who win the lottery.

Kat and I both said, "Thank you," but we said it so slowly, like we didn't want to burst this bubble of joy.

Then, I realized what this meant. Flash! I could buy Flash! "Thank you, thank you, thank you so much," I cried. "This is so unexpected."

Kat started saying thanks too as excitedly as me.

Mr. Elderbee waved for people to sit down. Wait. He wasn't done? How much more amazing could this day be? This was way, way better than turkey!

"One more thing, Kat and River. Before we move off to our dinner of thanks, our bank would also like to donate $5,000.00 to each of your clubs, so that you and your friends can continue with your good work. And Dudley Ellington Financial would also like to proudly donate $20,000 to the Sunnybrook Therapeutic Riding Program in your honor." Mr. Elderbee's smile deepened into a crescent as he reached out and shook each of our hands.

"River and Kat, would you please take a few minutes to tell all of us your story about the treasure hunt and how you found the buried map?"

Kat motioned for me to explain. I did. But I left off the part with the bear, although I really, really, really wanted to tell, so others could know how even more amazing and brave my best friend is.

The next day after school, I had one thing on my mind, *buying Flash.*

I never thought I'd have the money to buy him. Once the treasure was taken away and Flash was sold, I thought buying him was impossible and that I'd never get the chance. Life couldn't possibly be better. But when I raced up the drive, the whole farm was bustling with activity I'd never seen.

I heard Miss Carol say, "I found Freedom," she yelled into the barn as she trotted him in. "Two more to go."

My stomach dropped. I let my bike just fall in the dirt and I dashed up to her. "What's wrong? What happened?" Do you need help?" I galloped after her, waiting for an answer.

In the big barn, Kat was putting Morning Mist in her stall and she was crying.

"Some of the horses got out," Miss Carol explained. "And it's all *that* horse's fault." She pointed at Rocky, who looked guilty with his sad face and head drooped. "He's too wild for this farm! You need to get rid of him, Kat!"

"Don't even tell me that," Kat blubbered.

"How do you know *Rocky* did it?" I said, hoping there was some other explanation. "Did anyone see him do it?"

"No, but has the fence ever been broken like this before?"

"Well, when the branch fell on it," Kat reminded her. "You knew about that, right?"

"Yes, but there hasn't been a storm in days. *That* horse is nothing but trouble and has been since he got here. He stresses the other horses out. He shouldn't be here."

She stormed out and Kat broke down in sobs.

I patted her upper arm. "It'll be okay, Kat. We'll find the rest. Did Rocky get hurt from busting through the fence?"

"No, not that I could see. And he wasn't limping or anything. But I was frantic to help find the missing ones, so I didn't totally check him out."

"*I'll* check him out. He might need medical attention right away." I opened his stall and put his halter on and he walked right out. I looked his whole body over and felt his chest, back and legs with my hands. He didn't seem in discomfort or pain at all. I led him in each direction. "There's not a scratch on him. How could he bust the fence and not be hurt one bit?"

Kat shrugged. "I don't know. But it happened somehow. This is so, so bad. Everyone's mad at him and me and freaked out. You're going to be upset too."

"Me? Why would I … Wait? Who … who else is missing, Kat? Flash? Is it Flash?"

She nodded and big tears slid down her cheeks. "Yes, I'm sorry. We can't find Ginger …and … and Flash. You know how fast he runs, River. He could be the next town over by now."

I clutched her arm, encouraging her to run with me. "Come on." We jogged around the big barn and booked over to the pasture. I checked the break. I might be able to tell which horse did it by the prints or see which way

Flash went because his would be smaller. I looked for two front hoof prints that should've been in the dirt from the force of landing after such a crazed break. I didn't see any. I looked back at the fence and then the dirt, then the fence again. The top horizontal post looked like it had been bashed with a sledge hammer, not broken by horse legs because a lot of the wood pieces were inside the pasture not outside. "Someone did this," I said.

"That's crazy. Who would do that?"

"I have no idea." I scanned the ground around the fence and spun to leave when something caught the corner of my eye.

"Come on, River. This is wasting time. We need to look for Flash and Ginger."

"Wait a minute." I stooped to retrieve what I saw and held a cigarette butt in front of her eyes. "I told ya! Know any horses that smoke? That dude, who saw us with the treasure! *He* did this. I smelled smoke the other day. Flash kept turning his head to the tree line behind the big barn when we were working with Rocky. I had the feeling we were being watched, but I didn't see anything, and I thought I was imagining it or thinking crazy."

"Yeah, but we didn't get the treasure. We turned it in."

"But ... we are kind of rich. Our reward has been plastered all over the news." I looked to the woods and back at the ground.

Between horses and people, there was too much grass disturbed and crushed near the break and I couldn't make sense of anything. I followed the fence. After I passed the post, I ran my hand along the unbroken wood and saw a boot heel indentation in the soft dirt. I looked to the side of it and bent down and crawled in the dirt.

"What are you looking for? We need to go to the woods."

My heart sank when I saw what I hoped with all my might not to see. "Flash is not in the woods." The small crescent in the dirt was a partial footprint of one of Flash's hooves. It's not Star the pony's, since he's in the barn. Flash is the smallest horse.

"How do you know?" Kat bleated. She bopped on her heels in impatience and wrung her hands. "We need to go look, River."

Standing, I shouted, "I'm telling you, he's not in there."

"How do you know for sure?"

I pointed to the ground. "That's Flash's hoof mark. He took him. He took my horse!" I followed the whole fence line, and I found proof of exactly what I feared. I was right, totally right. This was the first time ever that I hated being right. "He led Flash out of here, I know it. You think I'm crazy?"

"No. I think you're brilliant, and I totally believe you."

I ran around the entire back of the fence, with

Kat following me. We were trying to find where he led him out.

She grabbed my arm and stopped. "Huh! Look, River."

I looked down and saw what she did. A tiny piece of carrot that probably fell out of Flash's mouth while he was gobbling up the treat from what he thought was a very kind stranger.

Kat covered her eyes and blubbered. "No. It's true! That crazy meanie took Flash! Do you think he'll hurt him?"

"Our reward was all over the news. I think he took Flash to blackmail us into giving him our money. Look for a note of some kind." We searched and searched.

Kat suddenly gasped and bashed my chest with her arm. "Oh no, oh no. Look." She pointed to the back of the big barn at some white object that wasn't supposed to be there. We raced up to it. A folded piece of paper was nailed to the wood. She carefully pulled it free.

Want your pony back?

Bring 100 GRAND to the park at midnight.

If you Tell ANYONE or Don't Deliver,

I'll HURL HIM into the Swollen River.

COME ALONE!

"By midnight?" I cried.

"A hundred thousand dollars? The banquet was just last night. I don't even have the money. I just have the check. Oh no! What are we gonna do! Poor Flash!"

"Don't worry. I'll think of something. I hope."

As scared as we were, we took the time to look for Ginger, while Kat and I came up with a plan. Luckily, Mr. M found her unharmed and put her back in her stall. We also looked for Flash all day for a good show.

At night, we both pretended to go to bed early, but we were really on the phone ironing out the details to get our horse back. She was so scared, but I told her to trust me.

At 11:45, we snuck out of our homes and met at the end of her driveway.

With the duffel bag on my shoulder, we tore down to the park as fast as we could on our bikes. He didn't say where to meet exactly, but it had to be big enough for a truck of some kind, so we stayed in the parking lot. The three-quarter moon lit up the park enough, but we put on a laser light show with our flash lights to calm our nerves while we waited for the guy to show up.

At 12:05, we heard the crunching of gravel and saw a box truck pulling into the lot.

"He's here," Kat whispered. I could feel her shaking next to me.

Kat and I looked at each other, hoping this would work.

VAIL & HOWELL

He stepped down from the cab of the truck and was immediately surrounded by cops that came out of the bushes and yelled, "Freeze."

I've seen enough cop shows to know that trying to pay a ransom by yourself never turns out well. So, I contacted this officer I know, who I've bought coffee for several times, and he helped me and Kat put this into motion.

The horsenapper put his hands up but then went for his waist and jerked out a gun.

"He's got a gun!" Kat screeched.

I shoved her behind me to shield her from bullets.

"Drop the gun," a cop yelled.

The guy fired a shot of fury or fear into the air then aimed a shaky hand at the line of police.

Kat screamed behind me and I recoiled and bumped into her. Shaking like mad, she clutched my shirt with both hands and leaned her head against my shoulder blades. She started praying out loud.

Suddenly tasered from a cop that had snuck up behind him, the crazed horsenapper shook for a few seconds and slumped awkwardly to the ground. Lifeless and not moving at all with his eyes open, he looked dead to me.

Kat cried, "Flash, Flash. Please be okay. I didn't know he was *that* dangerous!"

"Don't move! Don't move."

He definitely wasn't moving.

"He's down. We got him," an officer yelled. He knelt down and slid the gun across the pavement.

Two officers cuffed him, one secured the pistol, and another grabbed his keys and rushed to the back of the truck with a team.

We ran around to see too.

The police already had their guns drawn and told us to get back as it was eased open.

The warning wasn't needed. My heart sank, and I coughed out sobs with my fist over my lips.

The truck was totally empty.

Kat

The creepy guy who took Flash was Clyde Cranger, and he was literally crazy, well-known to the police. He lived alone on the other side of the mountain, and they said on the news he might've been desperate because his house was about to be foreclosed on. But in the twelve hours since we foiled him, no one could find Flash and the guy, now in a psychiatric facility, wasn't talking. Flash was totally missing. Police searched his whole property, and Flash was not on it.

I'd never seen River so freaked out, but being at my farm with Flash missing, or worse, was only upsetting him more, so he was staying away, trying to think up a plan.

He wasn't the only one. I called my Angels over in the morning for an emergency meeting to see if there was anything we could do to help the situation.

I was multitasking and working with Rocky in the round pen at the same time. I had Freedom just outside it with Posh leading him off and bringing him back. Rocky totally bought that this was just another lesson. Despite the glaring absence of Flash around here and a stressful night, he was calmer today.

"So, how do you like being rich?" Em asked, leaning against the metal rail from the outside.

"Well, it hasn't really hit me yet that I got a reward. I've been so worried about Flash."

"Think you'll take in more project horses?" Posh asked as she stroked Freedom's nose and held his lead line up near the halter.

"Awww, doubt it. Not now. I thought it was what I wanted, but I realized, at this point in time, I'm not really ready. A strong desire to help horses isn't enough. I need knowledge and more experience too. Rocky's a bigger problem than I can handle all by myself. He's doing okay in this game now, but I don't know how to help him for the long term. I put out an ad right before the banquet for someone to teach me tips, and I video chatted with a lady. She's excited to come over and work with us. But, right now, all I can think about is Flash."

Jacinda's voice cracked when she said, "What if ... something went really wrong, like Flash getting hurt, or *killed* even, in transport? He didn't have a proper horse truck. One slam on the brakes could've hurt him badly."

Emily blocked her ears. "No, no. Don't say that. Please. I don't want to picture poor Flash hurt."

"Me neither," Posh said. "This is so horrible. I can't even imagine what the poor baby is going through."

That made me break down and cry. He was still a baby. Not even a year old.

Posh led Freedom off again and came back.

"Maybe there's a place the cops haven't checked out yet," Emily said.

"It's a big, big world, Emily," I responded, "and Flash could be anywhere in it."

"What about Clyde's friends?" she said.

"What about them? You think someone would help that whackjob?" I asked.

She shrugged. "I don't know. Maybe. If he offered part of the reward." Emily edged down to sit on the ground and pulled her laptop out. She started clicking away.

"Whatcha doin', Em? What are ya thinking?" Leese asked.

"I'm just checking this guy out."

"Can you keep an eye on Rocky, Jacinda?" I said. "I need a little break. Want snacks and drinks?"

"Sure," everyone said.

Tory followed after me. "Need help?"

"Yeah? That'd be great."

We gathered everything quickly in the kitchen. I mixed canned lemonade in a plastic pitcher and got out a stack of cups.

When Tory and I came back out with the goodies, Posh was back with Freedom, and everyone was shouting over one another.

"What just happened? We were gone for two minutes." I cried. "Why's everyone arguing?"

"I have a good idea," Em said, "and Jacinda and Posh think it's a waste of time. And Tia and Leese are sticking up for me, so that's why everyone's upset."

"It *is* a good idea," Tia said, crossing her arms in defiance. "Not a dumb one. Not a waste."

"Let's hear *everyone* out and take a vote," I said. "What's your idea, Em?"

"This guy's an exterior painter and handyman and puts little ads out. In an article I found, it says he's well-known for his work, but he slacked when he didn't take his medication. He's gotten into some bar fights, and he used to do weird things like wear a ski mask in summer or put Easter eggs on his lawn, only to shout at kids to get off his property. Even though they're bizarre, it doesn't look like he ever did anything *this* crazy or bad."

"That's so sad," Posh said. "If only he had family to help him. Maybe he's totally alone."

"At least now," I said, "he's getting the help he needs. He was probably stressed out with the thought of losing his home and snapped. Maybe once he's treated, he'll tell us where Flash is. In the meantime, we've got to think of something else. Tell us more about your full plan, Em."

"Well, in the comment section on Facebook, someone posted they were glad he could do the job even while they were away on vacation. He sent pics and informed them of the progress the whole time. I looked them up and they live in town. Maybe there are other clients who are away now too."

"Okay. I see where you're going with this. It's not a bad idea." I looked at Jacinda and said, "Why don't we check it out? What's the problem?"

"Because," Jacinda said, "we can't go from house to house, checking the entire town. And besides, not everyone blabs that information online."

"Let Em dig a little more," Tory said. "What's the harm? Maybe she'll find a perfect avenue for us to follow."

Em said, "Hey, look. See? There's a note posted to one of the people he was working for and it says, '*When you get back, the job will be done*'."

"Yeah, good. It's a start," I said. "What if we just scroll down and see how many jobs he's got going? Maybe there are other notes about people out of town or something similar. River and I taught Flash to respond to our calls and whistles. If you and I go to some homes in town, Jacinda, we can call from the road. Maybe we'll get a response. It's better than sitting around doing nothing."

She nodded, agreeing to Emily's idea. It wasn't perfect, but it was *something* and a definite way we could help. "Okay. Is everyone in? Let's take a vote."

Leese said, "No one probably thought finding that lost treasure could be done, but Kat did it. I believe she can find Flash too."

So, it was unanimous.

"All right. Get some addresses for us, Em," Jacinda said.

"I guess *this* time," I said, "it's Jacinda and me going on a treasure hunt, but the treasure is Flash."

Emily got us five town addresses to check out. Our town wasn't *that* huge. Woods and farms took up the most space. I firmly believed we could do it.

The other Angels were going to continue working with Rocky while Jacinda and I checked out the creepy painter's in-town jobs. Emily wrote down directions for us, based on order.

When we biked over to the first address, I whistled from the road and called his name and got nothing. By the time we got to the second one, we were plum tired and aching from riding up and down all the hills. This was not as easy as we thought it would be, but we kept on going.

At the third house, an old blue colonial, we got off our bikes and I whistled again. I thought I heard something that sounded like Flash, so I had Jacinda be quiet and we both listened. Nothing but birds chirping. I whistled again and called his name and flowers bloomed in my chest. Oh my goodness. I think we did it. We actually did it. I think we found Flash!

We ran through a huge landscaped yard and in the back sat a shed where I heard whinnying. I could smell manure. The poor thing must be so hot, hungry and thirsty. I doubt that guy left him anything.

"Flash, Flash. Oh my goodness. Don't worry. We'll get you out, okay? I know you don't like small spaces."

Jacinda called the police as I opened the latch and wept at what I saw.

16

River

$\mathcal{L}$ying flat on my bed and staring at the ceiling in a fog because my brain was so utterly useless, I groaned when Kat's song came out of my phone. I didn't need to hear her crying. I've heard enough of it. I picked up anyway with a huff of annoyance. "Yeah? What do you want, Trouble?"

"Shut up, *Grouch*! I have an idea to search for Flash."

That got my attention. I shot straight up. "What! What? Tell me!"

"Get your butt over here, and I'll clue you in. Em thought of it."

"Okay. Okay. I'll be there in five." I flew out of bed, changed shirts with a cleaner one that I yanked off the floor. Once it was hugging my chest, I sniffed it. Good enough for this hunt or whatever this was. My blood was racing and buzzing with possibility. I hoped whatever plan she had was a decent one. It had to be better than my head load of nothing. At least she had an arrow of sure brilliance to follow. I ran out of my house like I was on fire and hopped on my bike. I'd never zipped there so fast. When I showed up, I scrunched my face in confusion.

All the girls were standing in a cluster. What on earth. They parted and that's when I saw Flash.

A tsunami of emotion hit me all at once and I choked up. I was so thrilled to see Flash, my blood sang and my spirit soared. I didn't even care that I lost tears in front of this group of girls. I didn't even try or care to fight it. "Flash. You're safe. You're here." I ran up and hugged him. I couldn't stop rubbing his head. "I'm glad you're okay, boy. Where on earth was he?" Flash nickered and nuzzled up against my feverish attention.

"Pee-uuuu. He was stuck in a shed all night and so smelly from horse poop," Tia said with a nose pinch.

"But, don't worry, we gave him a bath," Em said.

"And hay and water," Leese said. "He's all good and happy now. See?"

"How'd this happen?" I cried. "Where was this shed?"

"It was Em!" Tia cried with a clap. "She did it! She's awesome, so awesome. She did what the cops didn't even think to do."

"You did this, Em? You rock! How?" There was no limit

to what that girl could do. I hugged her, and she smiled like she'd just won a pageant. "You're my hero, Em. And Flash's. You saved me from a world of hurt."

"I just got the addresses online for work the horse thief was doing for Kat and Jacinda. They did the hard work in tracking Flash down. They called him from the street and he answered back, just like you taught him."

"You Angels are amazing. Thank you so much. This is the best thing I could imagine."

I heard Mrs. M, who walked up behind me say, "So, a little bird told me you wanted this horse?"

"I'm pretty sure it was a little Kat," Tia said with a mischievous chuckle.

Everyone cracked up, except Jacinda, who chastised her. "Tia. Don't be mean."

"Well, you call her little all the time."

"Yeah, but she's my best friend. It's a playful jab and she knows I love her. Plus, you're the smallest one of all of us."

I didn't care about them. I wanted my horse. "I do, I do, Mrs. M. More than anything. I'll pay whatever you want."

"By your dedication, I think you've more than demonstrated who he really belongs to."

"Yeah, but … I wanna pay you. I do. He represents money that could go to your very special and important program. I love it here, and I love him."

"River," she said, waving me off, but I wanted to do the right thing.

"Please. Mrs. M. I have the money now. My parents want me to save my money for college, but they said I can buy this one thing, as a blessing and treat, for being honest and honorable."

She nodded and looked around at all the smiling girls. "Okay. You pick the price."

"How about five grand? Does that sound fair?"

"Perfectly," she said with a big, warm smile. "I'm just so glad he's safe and sound now. Thank you so much for discovering right away that he was actually stolen and not missing somewhere in the woods. That saved his life, I'm sure."

"Maybe it did. Thank you, thank you, Mrs. M. Although I have a farm and the room to take him, would it be okay for me to board him here for a while? He still has so much equine skill to learn from the trainers and other horses."

"Of course. That would be wonderful. I love having that little grasshopper around. I did miss him when he was gone."

All the girls cheered, with Emily the loudest, screaming, "Yay!"

"Oh. If you wouldn't mind, and if Kat wouldn't, I'd really like to take Rocky too."

"You would?" Kat said with a sneer and a tone of complete shock. "Why? He's a nightmare at times."

"Well, yeah. I mean, Flash loves and needs the companionship of other horses. It makes him happy. And, aside from Freedom, Rocky is bonding with him best, so I think they'd make good buds for the long term, don't you?"

"Absolutely," Kat said with a big smile. "That would be so super amazing! They'd love it."

Mrs. M nodded. "Indeed. I think they'd make a fine pair, and I'm so impressed with your outlook and keen insight into equine instinct. I have no doubt in my mind you are the perfect owner for these horses."

"You can still help me with him, right, Kat?' I asked. "I can't do it alone."

"Yeah, of course. Neither can I. And about that, I also found someone who can come over and give us some behavioral mod pointers."

"Wow. That's great." I went back to hugging my little horse, then turned him out with some of the other geldings. He had fun playing and running with Rocky in the pasture the whole day. Yep. I could feel it in my spirit, that they'd definitely make a fine pair of companions and that *this* was my destiny. Kat and I watched the horses long after everyone left, until pink, purple and orange fingers pulled down a blue shade.

She whistled to call the horses back and they galloped to us like a synched troop.

My horses, my horses, my horses, rushed our way. I really liked the sound of that.

We started leading them back to the barns.

I looked at Kat and bit my lip. "Um, I didn't say this, and maybe should'a said it... but I ... didn't, 'cause I chickened out."

"Say what? When?"

I scratched my face and muttered, "Um, that you looked really beautiful in that red dress."

She gasped and looked at me with a glimmer of joy in her eyes. "Really beautiful? Wow. No one's ever said that to me, I mean, other than my parents. Um, thanks."

I impulsively kissed her cheek and said, "Thanks so much for finding my horse." I beamed at her building smile as I walked past and ahead of her.

"Uh ... yeah, no problem."

"Maybe you're not such *trouble* after all."

"Hmm. Maybe you're not either," she said with a laugh.

This was honestly the very best day of my life.

Kat

We sat scattered around Tory's purple explosion room, going over what we were going to say for our Stand Up Speak Out presentation, but it was missing a little bit of oomph, *I* thought anyway.

My stomach twitched like it held a dozen butterflies and I bit my lip. "Um, guys, I just have to say, that I did not at all appreciate you giving me an ultimatum to stay away from River. Yes, you all are important to me, and so is doing good deeds, but he's become one of my best friends, and blowing him off like I did made me feel literally sick and very sad."

"Sorry, Kat," Jacinda said with a cringe.

"Yeah, sorry," Tory said. "But *you* said he was the enemy. I just couldn't see the point of you spending so much time looking for footprints with a person you can hardly stand, and you were flopping in your responsibilities with us."

"I know, and I'm truly sorry that I flaked on the wristbands. I've changed my mind about River though. I was wrong about him and his motives, and I see that now. He just wanted to help people, and I saw it as him trying to one-up me. Instead of being out to best me, he's actually had my back, time and again, and I've had his."

"He's not a bad guy at all," Emily said. "I like him a lot."

"So do I," Tia said with a hop up from her seat on the floor. "He rocks!"

"Exactly. I agree," I said. "He *does* rock. So, I was thinking, what if we join forces with the Earth Helpers in our presentation? I was just talking to River. He's been bullied in school already and wants to do something about it. There's too much of it going on."

Leese nodded and said, "I love that idea. Let's do it."

Everyone nodded with delight on their faces.

"And maybe our clubs can work together more often," Emily said. "I really liked working in the garden with the Earth Helpers."

"Yeah, me too," Jacinda said. "I should've mentioned this before, but River wanted to join our club last fall, but I shot him down."

"I was there," Tia said. "I told you that was a bad idea."

"Quiet, Tia. I'm not finished. I did it because he and Kat

were fighting all the time, and *we* were arguing a lot too, so I thought it would never work. But I see that he has really good ideas. So do his club members. We started Angels Club to change the world, one meanie at a time, and intended to have more people join us in doing good deeds. I think today is the day we start opening our arms and spreading our wings, don't you?"

Everyone nodded and cheered excitedly. We didn't even have to vote because it was evidently a sure thing, and I couldn't have been more relieved. I was so glad they weren't mad at me and that I'd no longer have to choose between River and them. Each person was important to me and I didn't want to let anyone down. Even though I had money now, and a certificate celebrating my honesty, I'd never felt richer than this moment.

We called River and his friends over, and although his friends didn't want to speak at the presentation, they had good ideas that we could add to our talk.

When the day arrived, River's friends Greg and Sly were happy to join Leese at the table near our big poster where people could sign a Stand Up Speak Out pledge and receive wristbands to wear as a reminder to stop bullying.

We decided I'd speak first. I cleared my throat and tilted the mic down when I got up to it. "Hi. Thank you all for coming. Well, you pretty much had to, ha ha, since this is a mandatory assembly, but thank you for lending us your ears to this vital issue: bullying. At this school, we won't stand for it, and if you're with us, please go to the table in the hall, fill out a pledge card, and get a free Stand Up Speak Out wristband. Just on the second week of school, I saw my friend," I looked at River and smiled, "I mean, my *best* friend, getting bullied by some huge dude. He was bigger than me *and* my friend, so I felt powerless, like there was nothing I could do. Yeah, maybe that's hypocritical, since I'm talking about standing up, but that was a learning experience for me, so hopefully, it will be an educational experience for you. We're here to give you some tips on what you can do to feel empowered."

River went up and said, "Number 1. Don't ever be afraid to speak up. If you are bullied or see bullying going on, that's what the bully box in the main school office is for. You can either tell someone *or* anonymously report what you see or experience, and then a teacher or Principal Moran can check it out and deal with it. No one should have to put up with bullying or be afraid to walk their own school halls. Number 2. Don't give a bully any ammo. If you see it going on, don't encourage it by laughing or joining in on the taunting. If you are being bullied, try to stay cool. Physical retaliation as a response is a horribly bad idea. Try to talk yourself out of the situation, and if you can't, walk away as fast as you can."

"Number 3," Jacinda said. "Stand up for someone and be their voice. *I* was bullied, and felt so stupid and small, even though I'm a giant string bean, as you can clearly see, and I stopped bullying by standing up for the person who usually bullied me. Not only did that one act stop bullying in my former grammar school all together, I'm really good friends with her now. Can you believe it?"

Tory had to lower the mic because Jacinda's much taller. "I admit, *I'm* that bullying friend that Jacinda talked about, and I stopped doing it because Jacinda took the time to try to figure out why I might've been lashing out at her for no good reason. Even though it's no excuse, my sister died, and it rocked my world, and I was grumpy and mean for a long time. Remember the Abominable Snowman in *Rudolph the Red Nosed Reindeer* was only acting beastly because his tooth ached? Sometimes people are hurting or have a bad home life or are abused themselves, you don't know. So, Number 4 is, try to understand motivation and realize that bullies are human beings with flaws and scars, and maybe hidden turmoil. If you know someone who bullies, try to be a positive influence."

Posh rushed to the mic in her excitement and said, "Hi. Number 5 is to be kind, like an angelic hero. If you see someone being bullied or know someone who is being cyber-bullied, then reach out and be a friend. Your kindness could make a huge difference. You could be a lifeline to someone who's drowning in a sea of meanness. And that is all. Thank you so much for listening to our anti-bullying presentation. Like Kat said, you can fill out a pledge card and get a wristband…"

"Like these," we all cried with our arms together. "Stand up and speak out against bullying."

I beamed when the crowd of students stood on their feet and the room erupted in thunderous applause.

One horse, one person, one meal, one hug at a time, we were indeed changing the world as angelic do-gooders and earth helpers.

I really, really loved being me, Katarina McKinley, frizzy-haired shrimp that I am. Not only 'cause I was able to scare off a bear with my big fat mouth, but also because God blessed me with the best parents, friends, farm, and horse in the whole wide world. I spent so much time and energy looking for treasure in my own backyard, not seeing so clearly and sharply that I already had it.

Thanks for reading, Trackers!!!

ABOUT THE AUTHORS

COURTNEY VAIL In addition to writing quirky, twisty books for teens and adults, Courtney works from home as a graphic designer and book formatter. She's married to a *should-be-*famous comedian and has three kids who make her house LOUD and messy and do things like turn her veggie garden into Jurassic Park, but she thoroughly loves her life. She's a member of Authors Selling Books in Western Mass. Courtney is a *major* sports junky and loves to run, visit amusement parks (and ride all the roller coasters first), skate, cook, and watch standup or anything that cracks her up or makes her heart race or neck tingle. *Angels Club* is her first novel for kids.

SANDRA J. HOWELL is an avid horse enthusiast and was the first breeder in Massachusetts of the rare American Bashkir Curly horse. Her lifelong passion for Curly horses led her to write two Equine novels, *Spirit of a Rare Breed* and *Saving GiGi*. Howell, a college professor, has been a contributing writer, featuring the American Bashkir Curly horse, for Equine journals and magazines. She has been featured on television, radio talk shows and news media, and has received numerous letters from  Native Americans thanking her for promoting and advocating for their favored steed. Howell is a founding member of Authors Selling Books of Western Mass and is a member of the Independent Publishers of New England. Her novels are showcased at the *New England Equine Affaire* and promoted through many Equine organizations.

Learn more about the authors, merchandise and the *Angels Club* series at www.angelsclubkids.com and www.facebook.com/angelsclubnovel.

CPSIA information can be obtained
at www.ICGtesting.com
Printed in the USA
FFOW03n1541200218
45105738-45531FF

9 780984 558247